YOU BE THE JURY

Courtroom Collection

Marvin Miller

Inside illustrations by Bob Roper

SCHOLASTIC INC.

New York Toronto London Auckland Sydney
Mexico City New Delhi Hong Kong Buenos Aires

12 11 10 9 8 7 6 5 4 3 2 1   5 6 7 8 9 10/0

Printed in the U.S.A.   40

ISBN 0-439-77480-2

First compilation printing, January 2005

Contents

YOU
BE
THE
JURY

. .for Robby. . . . . . .

Order in the Court

LADIES AND GENTLEMEN OF THE JURY:
This court is now in session. My name is Judge John Denenberg. You are the jury, and the trials are set to begin.

You have a serious responsibility. Will the innocent be sent to jail and the guilty go free? Let's hope not. Your job is to make sure that justice is served.

Read each case carefully. Study the evidence presented and then decide:

INNOCENT OR GUILTY??

Both sides of the case will be presented to you. The person who has the complaint is called the *plaintiff*. He has brought the case to court.

The person being accused is called the *defend-*

ant. He is pleading his innocence and presents a much different version of what happened.

IN EACH CASE, THREE PIECES OF EVIDENCE WILL BE PRESENTED AS EXHIBITS A, B, AND C. EXAMINE THE EXHIBITS VERY CAREFULLY. A *CLUE* TO THE SOLUTION OF EACH CASE WILL BE FOUND THERE. IT WILL DIRECTLY POINT TO THE INNOCENCE OR GUILT OF THE ACCUSED.

Remember, each side will try to convince you that his version is what actually happened. BUT YOU MUST MAKE THE FINAL DECISION.

The Case of
the Dangerous Golf Ball

LADIES AND GENTLEMEN OF THE JURY:
If you are hit on the head by a golf ball while playing golf, there is very little that you can do legally. When you set foot on a golf course, you accept the risks that may occur. However, if you are standing in your house and are hit on the head by a golf ball, that is quite a different matter.

Such is the case before you today. Jason Compson, the plaintiff, is one of the homeowners of Green Acres Homes. He is suing the developer because a stray golf ball hit him while he was inside his house. Green Acres Development Corporation, the defendant, claims that Mr. Compson's injury is a complete fabrication, designed to harass them.

Mr. Compson has testified as follows:

"My name is Jason Compson. Two years ago, I bought one of the first homes in the Green Acres Housing Development. My home is one of sixty homes surrounding a private nine-hole golf course. Home buyers were invited to join the golf club, which was to be a private recreation center for the housing development."

During its first year, very few people joined the golf club. The club realized it would have to go out of business unless more people joined, so it announced it would change its policies and open the club to the general public.

To accommodate its plans, the club added an additional nine holes, clearing the trees near Mr. Compson's property.

Mr. Compson was upset. When he had purchased his home, he could sit on the patio overlooking the wooded land, barely seeing the golf course in the distance. When the new course was built, trees had been cleared, and he could now see the sixth tee which was fifty yards from his patio.

Before building the new course, Green Acres assured Mr. Compson it would be designed so that all golf shots would point away from his property. But it said nothing about the view. Besides seeing the sixth hole from his patio, Mr. Compson complained that when his windows were open, the constant chatter of golfers could be heard in his house.

Mr. Compson was so angry that he tried to get Green Acres to move the sixth tee. Mr. Compson claimed that the noise of the golfers calling, "caddy!" caused him mental distress, and he was in danger of bodily harm from a stray golf ball.

One day, Mr. Compson's prediction came true.

4

As he was in his den, hanging an expensive mirror, a golf ball shot through the window, hitting him on the head. He lost his grip and the mirror crashed on the mantle and fell to the floor.

Besides his injury, the mirror was completely shattered. The mantle was also heavily damaged.

Mr. Compson has sued Green Acres for his pain and suffering and for the cost to replace the broken mirror and repair the mantle. He further claims that the accident is proof of the unsafe location of the sixth tee and demands that Green Acres rebuild it farther away from his house.

EXHIBIT A shows the inside of Mr. Compson's den and the broken mirror. From the broken window, you can note the path the ball took directly across from where the mirror was being hung.

EXHIBIT B is a photograph of Mr. Compson, taken two days after the accident. Mr. Compson's lawyer asks you to note the large bandage and dark circles around his eyes. His injury took more than two weeks to heal.

The management of Green Acres presents a different view of the case. They claim that it was impossible for the accident to have occurred. They also state that Compson has repeatedly threatened the management.

A vice-president for Green Acres has testified: "I don't need any photographs or EXHIBIT B's to recognize Compson. I'd know him anywhere by his voice. At least once a day ever since the new course was built, Compson has been telephoning our office complaining about the noise. Compson also complained he would occasionally see a golfer in his backyard, looking for a stray ball and trespassing on his property."

Green Acres posted a guard near Compson's home but was never able to confirm Compson's complaints.

Green Acres argues that Mr. Compson's complaining was staged for the sole purpose of bothering the club. Green Acres offers as proof EXHIBIT C, showing the location of the sixth tee in relation to Compson's house. Because of the direction of the hole, it would be highly unlikely for a golfer to drive the ball into Mr. Compson's window.

Green Acres further claims that Compson had purposely faked the accident, and broke the mirror and mantle himself. They claim that Compson had no witness to the accident.

Green Acres requests the Court to dismiss Compson's charges, and asks that he be stopped from bothering the club and its golfers.

LADIES AND GENTLEMEN OF THE JURY: You have just heard the Case of the Dangerous Golf Ball. You must decide the merit of Jason Compson's claim. Be sure to carefully examine the evidence in EXHIBITS A, B, and C.

Could a golfer on the sixth tee have accidentally driven a ball through Jason Compson's window? Or did he stage the accident to dramatize his unhappiness with the new golf course?

EXHIBIT A

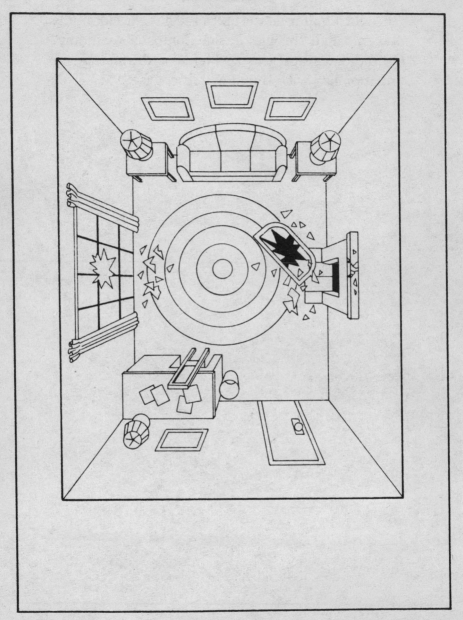

EXHIBIT B

EXHIBIT C

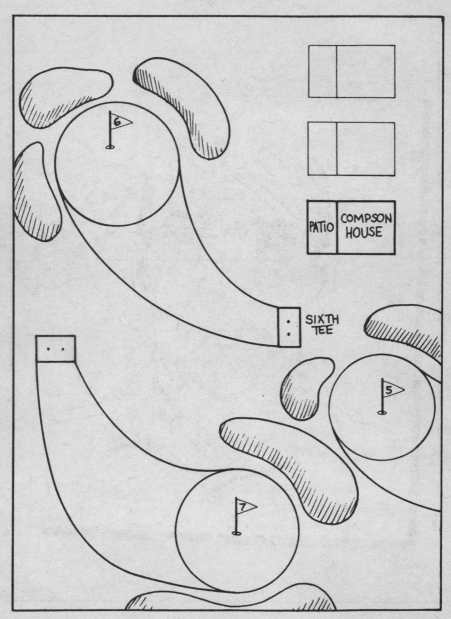

VERDICT

THE ACCIDENT WAS A FAKE.

The accident was faked by Jason Compson. EXHIBIT B shows Compson's forehead covered by a large bandage. If he had been hanging the mirror, his back would have been to the window. The injury would have been to the *back* of his head.

The Case of
The Rotten Apples

LADIES AND GENTLEMEN OF THE JURY:
A person does not have the legal right to commit a criminal act while defending his own private property.

That is the point of law you must keep in mind today. Arthur Hallow, the plaintiff, admits that he trespassed on the farm property of Farmer Frost, the defendant. But Mr. Hallow charges that when he did so, he was viciously attacked by Mr. Frost, and that Frost broke Hallow's arm. Arthur Hallow is suing Farmer Frost for assault, and is asking for money to pay his medical bills. Farmer Frost says that Arthur Hallow is lying.

Arthur Hallow has testified to the following:

"On the evening of October 5, around six o'clock, I was hiking along Somerset Road. I passed the woods that mark the start of Farmer Frost's property. I know Farmer Frost lives there, but there's no sign or anything that says to keep out.

"Along the edge of the woods is a path leading to the Frost farmhouse. I started down the path because it also leads to the Frost orchard. Everyone knows Farmer Frost has the best apples around. I planned to fill my knapsack with apples. I've done it lots of times before and nothing ever happened."

After Hallow reached the orchard, he leaned against a tree to rest. Suddenly he yelled out loud. He had backed up against a patched tree and could feel the wet tar seeping through his shirt.

I refer again to the actual testimony of Arthur Hallow when questioned by his attorney. First the question and then the answer:

Q What happened after you yelled?

A I started picking apples from the ground and filling my knapsack. Most of the apples on the ground were rotten.

Q Did you climb any of the trees?

A I was about to when I heard a voice behind me. It was Old Frosty, and he shouted for me to stop.

Q What was the name you just used?

A Old Frosty. That's what everyone calls Farmer Frost because he's so mean and has a nasty temper.

Q Then what happened?

A I turned around and saw he was pointing a gun at me. I was frightened and promised I would give him back his apples.

Q What was his reply?

A He was upset. He put down his gun and attacked me. I tried to run, but he grabbed me from behind in a bear hug. I dropped the apples. He grabbed my left wrist and twisted it behind my back.

Q Did you attempt to defend yourself?

A No. I cried for him to stop. He was hurting my arm. The more I yelled, the more he pulled. Suddenly my arm went limp and a sharp pain shot through it.

Q When did Frost let go?

A When he realized what he had done, he backed away and picked up his rifle. He kept it pointed at me until the police arrived.

Arthur Hallow was rushed to the local hospital where X-rays revealed a broken arm. He wants Farmer Frost to pay for the medical bills.

Farmer Frost presents a completely different explanation of what happened. First of all, he states that his property is indeed marked. EXHIBIT A is the "No Trespassing" sign found by the police near the path leading to Farmer Frost's house. The police have said it was clearly visible from Somerset Road.

In addition, Farmer Frost has made the following statement:

"I was just sitting down to dinner when I heard a loud cry from out in the orchard. It sounded like someone was hurt, so I immediately called the police."

EXHIBIT B is the police record of this call.

As he waited for the police, Frost heard another yell followed by a thud. He peered out the window and saw Arthur Hallow slowly picking himself up from the ground. Presumably he had fallen from a tree. The youth held his arm and began running toward Somerset Road.

Frost took his gun and ran after the trespasser. He quickly caught up with him and held him at gunpoint. Moments later, the police arrived. EXHIBIT C is a photograph taken at the scene.

Farmer Frost claims he had nothing to do with Arthur Hallow's broken arm, and he refuses to pay the medical expenses.

LADIES AND GENTLEMEN OF THE JURY: You have just heard the Case of the Rotten Apples. You must decide the merit of Arthur Hallow's claim. Be sure to carefully examine the evidence in EXHIBITS A, B, and C.

Is Farmer Frost guilty of the assault as charged? Or did Arthur Hallow make up the entire story?

EXHIBIT B

D.D.5

CRIME CLASSIFICATION	POLICE DEPARTMENT REPORT
TRESPASSING	

NAME OF COMPLAINANT	ADDRESS
FARMER FROST	5 Somerset Road

6:40 P.M. phone call. Complainant heard noise outside his house on the grounds of his apple grove. Believes he heard someone yelling.

Dispatched Car 43 to location.

Greg Baldwin

OFFICER ON DUTY

EXHIBIT C

VERDICT

ARTHUR HALLOW WAS LYING.

If Frost had grabbed Hallow from behind as the youth claimed, tree tar would have been smeared on Frost's shirt. In EXHIBIT C, Frost's shirt is perfectly clean.

The Case of
The Squashed Scooter

LADIES AND GENTLEMEN OF THE JURY:

If the driver of a car accidentally damages another vehicle that is improperly parked, the driver is not responsible for any damage.

While Archy Leaf, the plaintiff, was shopping at Cherry Hill Mall, his motor scooter was run over by a car driven by Butch Brando, the defendant. Mr. Leaf charges that Mr. Brando purposely ran over the scooter to get even with him. Butch Brando says he is not responsible for the accident and will not pay for the damages.

Archy Leaf has given the following testimony:

"It was Saturday afternoon, July 24. I rode my motor scooter over to the Cherry Hill Mall and parked in an empty parking space. I stopped in at the Card Shoppe for a birthday card for my girl friend. Then I went into Rush Records. My favorite group, Engine Summer, had a new tape out, and I wanted to see if the store had it.

"I remember passing my motor scooter on the way to Rush Records. It was parked upright."

Leaf was in the record store for about five

minutes when he heard a loud crunch and ran outside. To his horror, he saw his scooter lying crushed under the wheels of Butch Brando's car. Several shoppers gathered around the accident, but there were no eyewitnesses.

EXHIBIT A is a map of Cherry Hill Mall with the path Archy Leaf took from the card store to the record shop.

EXHIBIT B is a photograph of the accident scene. You will note the scooter's tangled wreckage under the car.

Archy Leaf continued with his testimony:

"My scooter was properly parked, I'm sure of that. But more important, this was no accident, I can tell you. Butch Brando was out to get me. He's been mad at me for the past two weeks. We both have summer jobs working at Burger Palace. Butch has been coming back from lunch later and later every day, and I finally had to tell the boss. There's too much work for me to handle all by myself.

"The day after I spoke with the boss, Butch came up to me in the parking lot. 'You won't get away with this,' he said. 'I'll get even no matter what. Just wait and see. You'll be *shaking* like a leaf, Leaf, before I'm through with you.' I'm sure Butch Brando ran over my scooter on purpose."

Mr. Leaf seeks payment for damages of $280.00.

Butch Brando has presented a very different version of what happened. I will now read from

21

his testimony. First the question from his attorney and then Mr. Brando's answer:

Q Where were you on the afternoon of Saturday, July 24?

A I was driving around in my car. I love my car. There's no way I would ever do anything that might put a dent in it.

Q When you drove into the mall, what did you see?

A The parking lot was crowded with cars. There were a few motorcycles and scooters parked, but I didn't see Archy's scooter anywhere, if that's what you mean. I finally found a narrow parking space between a van and another car. The van was hogging part of the space.

Q Did you see a motor scooter in that space?

A I certainly did not. At least not from my view behind the wheel. The front of my car sticks out pretty far.

Q Then what happened?

A I drove slowly into the space. All of a sudden I heard something crunch under the wheels of my car. I immediately put on the brakes.

Q How long have you known Archy Leaf?

A Archy and I are old friends. We used to be in Mrs. Kowalski's class back in grade school. He's kind of a nervous little guy, you know what I mean? So I like to tease him, but he knows I'm only kidding. I'd never do anything to hurt him.

Mr. Brando further stated that when he drove his car into the parking space he saw two young boys running away from the scene. He suggests that if the scooter was not carelessly parked flat on the ground by Leaf himself, then the two boys may have knocked it down.

Witnesses have stated that there *were* vandals at the mall at the time, spraying shaving cream across the windows of several cars. Brando offers as proof EXHIBIT C, which is a police complaint by a shopper whose window was sprayed by vandals around the time of this accident.

Butch Brando says that the scooter was lying *flat* on the parking space ground. Since it was parked improperly he was unable to see it. Mr. Brando requests the charges against him be dismissed because the accident was due to Leaf's own carelessness.

LADIES AND GENTLEMEN OF THE JURY: You have just heard the Case of the Squashed Scooter. You must decide the merit of Mr. Leaf's claim. Be sure to carefully examine the evidence in EXHIBITS A, B, and C.

Did Butch Brando knowingly drive his car over Archy Leaf's motor scooter? Or was it an accident?

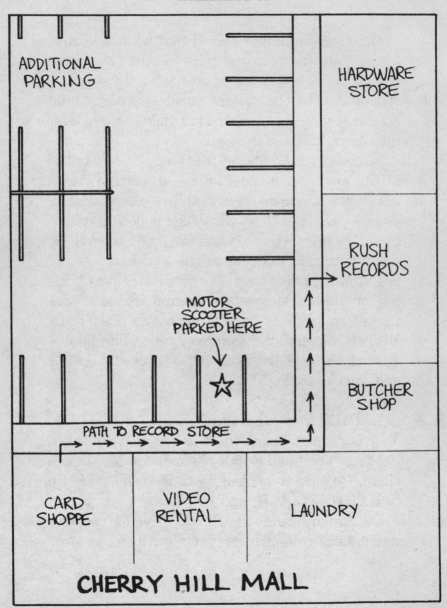

EXHIBIT C

EXHIBIT C

D.D. 5

CRIME CLASSIFICATION	POLICE DEPARTMENT REPORT
VANDALISM	

NAME OF COMPLAINANT	ADDRESS
MS. SANDRA HELFANO	844 Wingate Terrace

11:17 A.M. Complainant was shopping inside
Green's Hardware Store. Claims that two young
boys were creating a disturbance in the parking
lot of the Cherry Hill Mall. She saw them spraying
shaving cream across the windows of cars.

Greg Baldwin
OFFICER ON DUTY

VERDICT

BRANDO SQUASHED
THE SCOOTER ON PURPOSE.

The motor scooter, shown in EXHIBIT B, was crushed under the *rear* wheels of Butch Brando's car. If, as Brando had claimed in his testimony, he stopped the car immediately when he heard the crunch, the motor scooter would have been under the *front* wheels. Brando purposely ran over Leaf's scooter.

The Case of
The Wrong Bag

LADIES AND GENTLEMEN OF THE JURY:

A person who is found with stolen property is not necessarily a thief.

Keep this in mind as you go over the facts in this case. Since we are in criminal court today, the State is the accuser. In this case, the State, represented by the district attorney, has accused John Summers of robbing Kay's Jewelry Store. John Summers, the defendant, has pleaded innocent and claims that his arrest is a mistake.

The State called the owner of Kay's Jewelry Store as its first witness. She has testified as follows:

"My name is Wendy Kay, and I own Kay's Jewelry Store in Martinville. I was working alone in the store on Wednesday afternoon, December 2, when a man walked in. It was exactly 3:30. I noticed the time because I had just put a new collection of diamond watches from Switzerland on display. I noticed the man because he had a handkerchief over his face. I thought that was odd until I also noticed the outline of a gun projecting from his pocket. That's when I got scared."

The man ordered Wendy Kay to empty a case of jewels and all the store's cash into a black bag. The robbery took only minutes, and the thief escaped on foot.

At four o'clock the next afternoon, John Summers entered the lobby of the Bristol Hotel and walked over to the luggage checkroom. He pointed to a black bag, which the bellman gave him. As he handed the bellman a tip, a hotel detective noticed that Summers' bag matched the description of the bag used in the jewelry store robbery. He arrested Summers and called the police.

When the police opened the bag and emptied its contents, a look of shock and surprise spread over Summer's face. Inside was the stolen jewelry.

John Summers was dumbfounded. He claimed he had pointed to the wrong bag in the hotel checkroom. This bag was not his, he said, but an identical twin belonging to someone else. His own bag contained a blue toothbrush and underwear, and it was locked.

The police returned to the luggage checkroom and questioned the bellman. The man thought there might have been two bags in the checkroom, although a second black bag was nowhere to be found.

EXHIBIT A is a picture of the bag and jewelry.

John Summers claims that he checked an identical bag and that he mistakenly picked up this bag from the luggage room.

The State has drawn your attention to the shape of this bag, its handle, and lock. The State submits that this is an unusual-looking bag, and that it is very unlikely, if not impossible, that another bag looking just like it would be checked into the same hotel on the same day.

The State also presented EXHIBIT B, a list of the contents of John Summers' pockets at the time he was arrested. His wallet contained $710 in cash, a sizable sum for a person spending only one night in town. The State alleges that the $710 in Summers' wallet is the money stolen from the jewelry store.

No gun was found in Summers' pocket. The State claims a simple explanation. John Summers robbed Kay's Jewelry Store by pretending the object in his pocket was a gun. In reality, it was only his pointed finger.

On the basis of all this evidence, John Summers was accused of the jewelry store robbery.

John Summers has given the following testimony:

"My visit to Martinville was supposed to be a simple overnight trip. Every year around this time, the Martinville Museum has its annual art sale, and I wanted to buy a painting. I just started collecting art last year. I may not know a lot about art, but I know what I like. I've already got two of those pictures of the sad-looking kids with the big eyes. But this time I wanted something really stupendous to go over the sofa in the living room. Maybe something with some purple in it to match the drapes. I saved up more than eight hundred bucks to buy a painting this trip."

Summers' schedule was easy to reconstruct. He arrived by bus on Wednesday morning and checked into the Bristol Hotel. The Museum opened at noon. Mr. Summers was one of the first persons to enter the Museum. He spent the entire afternoon there. But to his disappointment, he could not find any artwork he liked.

EXHIBIT C is a torn Museum ticket stub for the day in question. The Museum hours were noon to four o'clock. The robbery of Kay's Jewelry Store took place at 3:30. While there was no witness who can testify he saw John Summers in the Museum the entire time, the stub shows he indeed visited the Museum.

When the Museum closed, John Summers went back to his hotel, disappointed his trip was in vain. The following day, he checked out of the hotel at noon. Since his bus did not leave until later that day, Summers locked his black bag, checked it in the hotel's luggage checkroom, and went sightseeing. Later he returned to pick up his bag, and he was promptly arrested.

John Summers claims that he is the victim of

an unfortunate coincidence.

LADIES AND GENTLEMEN OF THE JURY:
You have just heard the Case of the Wrong Bag.
You must decide the merit of the State's accusation. Be sure to carefully examine the evidence
in EXHIBITS A, B, and C.
Did John Summers rob Kay's Jewelry Store?
Or had he indeed picked up the wrong bag?

EXHIBIT A

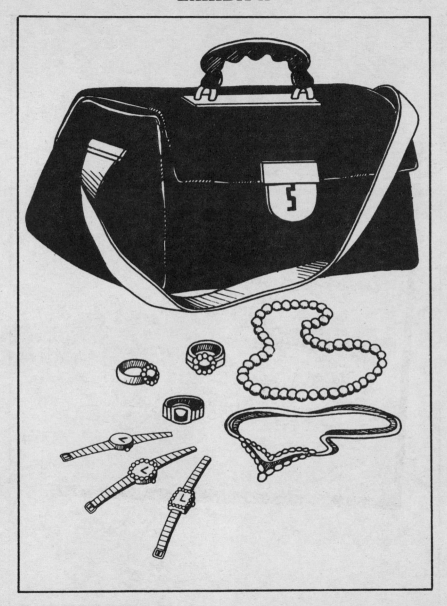

POLICE (PD) DEPARTMENT

JOHN SUMMERS

Contents of pockets

1. Wallet contents:
   a. $710.00 cash
   b. Driver's License
   c. Master Card
2. Handkerchief
3. Comb
4. $1.25 in coins
5. Chewing Gum
6. Ticket Stub (Martinville Museum)
7. Hotel Bill

EXHIBIT C

VERDICT

JOHN SUMMERS WAS LYING.

John Summers claimed that the bag he stored in the checkroom was *locked*. But the contents of his pockets in EXHIBIT B showed he had no key. Summers was lying. He had indeed robbed Kay's Jewelry Store, and the bag with the jewelry was his.

The Case of
the Missing Will

LADIES AND GENTLEMEN OF THE JURY:
People write wills so that when they die their
wealth can be passed along according to their
instructions. A person may change his or her will
as many times as he or she likes. However, it is
the last will that is considered to be legal.

Stanley Woot was a wealthy businessman and
inventor. He had two children, Barbara and Stan,
Jr. When he died last July, his will revealed that
he had left all his money to his daughter Barbara.
Stan, Jr. has contested this will. Stan, Jr. claims
that he has discovered a later will which states
that he and Barbara should share their father's
money equally.

Barbara Woot has given the following testimony:

"As you all know, my father was very successful
all his life. He made his first fortune at the age
of nineteen by inventing the little metal band that
holds the eraser onto the end of a pencil. The only
unsuccessful part of his life was his personal life.
I'm speaking about my younger brother, Stan,
Jr.

"Stan, Jr. was always a problem child. As he grew older, he would do anything to avoid work. He seemed to think that life was one big party. It always hurt me to see how unhappy he made my father."

The relationship between father and son grew strained, and five years ago Stanley Woot cut off all financial support. Stan, Jr. then moved to another part of the state, and the two rarely saw each other.

In July, Stanley Woot died following a long illness. The following day, the family's lawyer met the children in the library of the Woot mansion for the reading of the will. In it, Stanley Woot had left his entire fortune to his daughter Barbara.

Stan, Jr. protested. He claimed that a week before his father's death, his father contacted him. The elder Woot knew his illness was serious and proposed they reestablish their relationship. In return, Stan, Jr. promised he would change his idle ways. The elder Woot then drafted a new will.

Barbara was skeptical when she heard this story. But Stan, Jr. sought to prove that a newer will existed.

The evening following the reading of the will, Stan, Jr. searched through his father's house. By morning he had discovered an envelope containing a *new* will in his father's desk drawer. The new will stated that Stan, Jr. and Barbara should share their father's fortune equally.

Barbara Woot testified further:

"Stan, Jr. says he has changed his ways, but he has not. In fact, just before our father's death, Stan, Jr. flew to Paris for the weekend and went on a shopping spree. He charged everything to Dad's account."

When Stanley Woot received the bills, he became so angry that he immediately published a notice in newspapers around the world. The official notice, which disavows responsibility for his son's actions, appeared just two weeks before Stanley Woot died. This notice is EXHIBIT A.

Barbara Woot says that Stan, Jr. is lying: There was no change in his relationship with his father, and the will he claims to have discovered is a fake.

Stan, Jr. has testified as follows:

"It's true, my father and I were never close. Ever since I can remember, we've argued about something, mostly money and my friends. Maybe if he hadn't been so wrapped up in his business, things would have been different. . . .

"The week before he died, my father called me. He had been sick for a long time and knew he didn't have much time left. He told me he wanted us to work out our problems, he was sorry he'd failed as a father, and he asked me to forgive him."

Stan, Jr. says that he visited his father, not once but several times during the last week of Stanley Woot's life. Testimony of the family housekeeper, which is entered as EXHIBIT B, is offered as proof that father and son were again on good terms.

Although she did not overhear their actual conversations, the housekeeper could detect no sign of anger between them. In contrast, the housekeeper stated that in earlier years, Stan, Jr. and his father quarreled bitterly — and loudly.

Stan, Jr. has told the court:

"You've heard that my father and I finally mended our relationship. Naturally, I was shocked when the will was read and in it my father left everything to my sister Barbara. Since my father had told me he was making out a new will, I thought maybe he hadn't had a chance to give it to his attorney. I decided to see if I could find the new will at his house. The next morning, while I was searching through his desk, I found the envelope containing the new will. As you can see, my father has asked that his estate be divided equally between Barbara and me."

EXHIBIT C is the new will itself.

LADIES AND GENTLEMEN OF THE JURY: You have just heard the Case of the Missing Will. You must decide the merit of Stan, Jr.'s claim.

Be sure to carefully examine the evidence in EXHIBITS A, B, and C.

Is the will found by Stan, Jr. the last will and testament of Stanley Woot? Or is it a fake?

ANNOUNCEMENTS

BE A MILLIONAIRE
New easy method.
Works while you sleep.
Call 355-1212 after midnight.

**STOP SMOKING
LOSE WEIGHT
See results fast.
"IT'S ALL DONE
WITH MIRRORS"
For more information call
976-5858**

I, Stanley Woot,
will not be responsible
for any debts of Stan Woot, Jr.

**MUSIC 'N THINGS
THE FUN HOME PARTY
Sell band instruments**

EXHIBIT B

STATEMENT OF GRETA BURROWS

I have been the housekeeper for the late Stanley Woot for fourteen years. During this period, I have been in the house several times when he was visited by his son, Stan Jr.

The relationship between father and son was not very friendly. Over the past several years, whenever the two met, their talks always ended in Stanley Woot yelling at his son and his son yelling back. Each time, Stanley Woot accused his son of being lazy with no ambition to make anything of himself. Each meeting ended with Stan Jr. leaving the house in tears and Mr. Woot telling his son never to come back.

But several times a year, months after their fight Stanley Woot would telephone his son and ask him to come to the house again. When he did, the fighting would soon start.

During the week preceding the death of Stanley Woot, he again called his son. When Stan Jr. came to the house, it was the first time I was there that the two of them did not have a bitter argument. They met for an hour behind the closed door of Stanley Woot's den. I did not overhear the conversation, but I can state that they definitely did not yell at one another.

During the final week, there was nothing I saw or heard that would lead me to believe they were angry with one another.

(signed) Greta Burrows

(notarized)

sworn to me this 21 day of

July, 1985.

43

EXHIBIT C

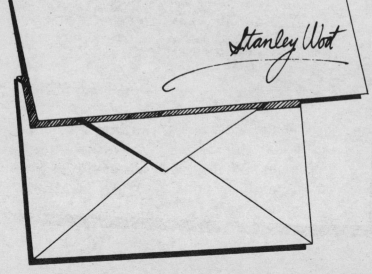

July 7, 1985

To whom it may concern;

This is my last will. I give
and bequeath to my daughter Barbara
Woot and my son Stan Woot Jr., to be

divided equally, in complete and
perfect ownership, all my rights
and property of every kind and
nature, whether real or personal.

Stanley Woot

VERDICT

THE NEW WILL IS A FAKE.

The will that was found by Stan, Jr. in EX-
HIBIT C is folded once. But it is too large to fit
into the envelope. Stan, Jr. had typed the will,
forged his father's signature, grabbed an envelope, and brought them to the lawyer. But he
neglected to make sure the will fit inside the
envelope.

The Case of
the Fast Getaway

LADIES AND GENTLEMEN OF THE JURY:
Just because a man has been found guilty of a
crime once before, this does not mean he will be
a criminal forever.

The State, represented by the district attorney,
has accused Frank Carson of robbing Party Poopers, Inc. Frank Carson, the defendant, says that
he is innocent.

The State called Glinda Harris as its first
witness:

"My name is Glinda Harris. I'm the office
manager of Party Poopers, Inc. We make and sell
all kinds of party supplies and novelties. You
know those little bottles that pop and shoot out
confetti when you pull the string? Those are our
party poppers. Our most famous item is our Party
Pooper whoopee cushion. We've sold nearly a
million this year alone.

"On Friday morning, October 28, I arrived at
our office on the fifth floor of Glendale Plaza at
eight o'clock. I like to get to work early so I can
prepare the office for the day.

46

"As I was opening the office safe there was a knock on the back door. I thought it was an employee who had forgotten their key, so I opened the door."

Glinda Harris was confronted by a man, about six feet tall, wearing a bulky blue down jacket, and holding a knife. A yellow paper party hat was pulled down over part of his face.

The intruder grabbed Glinda Harris from behind. Warning her not to scream, he dragged her over to an exposed water pipe and chained her left arm to it. The robber emptied the safe of $2,000 in cash, stuffing it into a paper trick-or-treat bag he was carrying. He threw down the knife and fled, escaping in a green and white sports car.

The police later found that the realistic-looking knife was actually made out of rubber.

The following day, a man identified as Frank Carson was stopped while traveling 60 miles per hour in a 35 mile zone. His facial features, clothes, and car were similar to those described by Glinda Harris. EXHIBIT A is a copy of the burglar's description which Glinda Harris gave to the police.

Based on this description, Frank Carson was placed under arrest. When Carson was arrested, the police found eight hundred dollars in cash hidden in his left shoe. They also found a notice in his car that he owed his bank $1,000. The State contends that it seems suspicious that Carson would be carrying $800 in cash while being unable to pay the $1,000 bank loan. The State argues that the cash in Carson's shoe was from the robbery.

Further investigation by the police turned up the fact that Frank Carson had been arrested before. EXHIBIT B is information taken from Frank Carson's permanent criminal record. The State has asked you to note the similarity between these earlier crimes and the robbery at Party Poopers. Based on all this evidence, the State asks that you find Frank Carson guilty as charged.

Frank Carson says that he is innocent. He has testified as follows:

"Yes, it's true. I used to be a bad character. But that was a long time ago. Since then I've gone straight. These days I'm a consultant for the TV networks. You may wonder what experience I have that would interest a TV company. Well, whenever they're doing a crime show, they call on me — to make sure all the crimes look realistic."

Frank Carson's lawyer has also challenged the description by Glinda Harris that led to the arrest. He claims that the information she gave was too general to prove that Frank Carson was the robber. Many people could fit the description given by Mrs. Harris. To further cast doubt on the description, Frank Carson's lawyer has presented

48

EXHIBIT C, a diagram of the room where the robbery was committed.

You will note that the safe is on the opposite side of the room from the water pipe where Glinda Harris was chained. Thus the robber probably had his back to Mrs. Harris most of the time he was in the room.

Because of the weaknesses in Glinda Harris' case, Frank Carson asks that the charges be dropped.

LADIES AND GENTLEMEN OF THE JURY: You have just heard the Case of the Fast Getaway. You must decide the merits of the State's accusation. Be sure to carefully examine the evidence in EXHIBITS A, B, and C.

Is Frank Carson guilty of robbing Party Poopers, Inc.? Or was the robbery committed by someone else?

EXHIBIT A

D.D. 5

CRIME CLASSIFICATION	POLICE DEPARTMENT REPORT
ROBBERY	

NAME OF COMPLAINANT	ADDRESS
GLINDA HARRIS	42 Glendale Plaza

Be on the lookout for suspect wanted in connection
with robbery at Party Poopers, Inc.

Description:

     age: 25-35

     height: 6 feet

     hair: color unknown

     eyes: blue or green

     weight: heavy build

When last seen was wearing: blue down jacket,
blue jeans, running shoes.

Escaped in green and white two-door sports car.

Make and model unknown.

Greg Baldwin

OFFICER ON DUTY

EXHIBIT B

INFORMATION FROM CRIMINAL RECORD

Frank Carson

This man twice convicted on larceny and conspiracy to commit larceny on several counts.

$1,000 stolen from Greenbatch Supply Company, NYC at knifepoint on March 12, 1972. Suspended sentence.

$5,000 stolen at knifepoint from Willis Knitting Factory, Ontego, NY May 20, 1974. Served two years at Bradford NY prison. No record of additional arrests.

EXHIBIT C

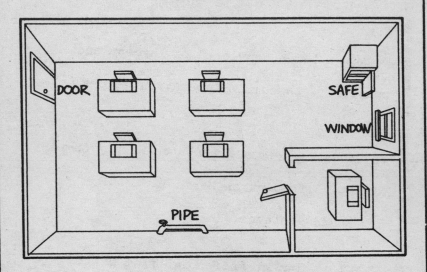

5TH FLOOR OFFICE
PARTY POOPERS, INC.

VERDICT

FRANK CARSON
WAS NOT THE ROBBER.

Had Glinda Harris been chained to the pipe, she would not have been able to see out the window (see EXHIBIT C) to describe how the burglar escaped or the color of his car. Mrs. Harris had fabricated the robbery in order to cover her own theft.

The Case of
the Power Blackout

LADIES AND GENTLEMEN OF THE JURY:
A company that provides a public service, such as a power company, has special responsibilities. When the service fails, the company is responsible for any damages that may happen.

Keep this in mind as you decide the case before you today. Mel Mudd, the plaintiff and owner of Mudd's Diner, claims that a power failure lasted sixteen hours and he was unable to serve his customers. Mr. Mudd wants to be paid for this lost business. Allied Utilities, the defendant, is a power company that provides electricity and gas to the people in Fairchester County. Allied Utilities admits to the power failure. But it claims to have repaired it three hours after it was reported.

Mel Mudd has given the following testimony:

"My name is Mudd. I'm the owner of Mudd's Diner. On Thursday, February 16 at 9:30 P.M., just as I was about to close up for the night, the lights went out. Do you know that old joke: Where was Thomas Edison when the lights went out? Well, the answer is: In the dark. And that's exactly where I was, too. I immediately called the power company and was assured the power would be restored promptly."

Mr. Mudd returned to his diner the following morning, opened the back door and flipped on the light switch. The room was totally dark.

He telephoned the power company several times, and each time the line was busy. After posting a "closed" sign on the front of the diner, Mudd returned to the back room and tried to telephone the company again. The line was still busy.

Mr. Mudd kept phoning the utility company and after two hours finally got through. The company told him they had fixed the problem the night before, but they promised they would send a repairman right away.

It took two hours for the repairman to arrive. By that time, Mr. Mudd had turned away the noon lunch crowd.

The repairman again checked the outside cable. He tightened the couplings but found nothing to indicate further repairs were needed. When the repairman went back to the diner to report his findings, the lights were on in the back room.

Mr. Mudd insisted the second visit was necessary to repair the lost power because the work had not been done properly the night before. He telephoned Allied Utilities and told them he planned to sue the company for lost business. A supervisor arrived at the diner in five minutes.

EXHIBIT A shows the lost business at Mudd's Diner during the time Mudd claims he had no power. You will note on that day he had only $146.35 in business. Entries for other days show he usually had up to $450.00 worth of business. This is the amount Mudd seeks from the utility company — $450.00.

Mel Mudd was extremely angry when the supervisor arrived at the back room of the diner. The man assured Mudd the power failure had been fixed the night before. Mudd strongly disagreed.

Allied Utilities enters as EXHIBIT B the repair work-order for the diner. This is a record kept for each customer complaint. You will note that the first call came in at 9:35 P.M. The repair order shows that the power failure lasted only three hours during the time the diner was closed. Power was claimed to have been restored by 12:36 A.M.

The company also enters EXHIBIT C, a photograph of the back room that was taken shortly after the supervisor arrived. You will note that the supervisor is holding up a light bulb. He had found it in a wastebasket in the diner's back room. Tests have shown this bulb is burned out and no longer in working order.

The company contends that while its repairman was outside checking the power the second time, Mudd somehow realized he may have been mistaken about the power failure. The light in the back room had failed to go on because of a burned out bulb. Mr. Mudd then replaced the bulb with a new one but said nothing to the company so he could sue them for lost business. Allied Utilities refuses to pay the money Mel Mudd has requested.

LADIES AND GENTLEMEN OF THE JURY: You have just heard the Case of the Power Blackout. You must decide the merit of Mel Mudd's claim. Be sure to carefully examine the evidence in EXHIBITS A, B, and C.

Should Allied Utilities pay Mr. Mudd for the income he lost during the power failure? Or did Mudd know that the power had been restored?

EXHIBIT A

GROSS RECIEPTS
WEEK OF FEB. 12

DATE	BREAKFAST 6-11	LUNCH 11-5	DINNER 5-9	TOTAL
2/12	93.25	116.40	170.50	380.15
2/13	123.60	88.25	225.80	437.63
2/14	85.25	116.45	248.70	450.40
2/15	47.65	93.85	286.45	427.95
2/16	48.10	106.75	254.05	408.90
2/17	—	20.00	126.35	146.35
2/18	94.45	123.20	204.20	421.85

WEEKLY TOTAL - $2,694.10

EXHIBIT B

ALLIED ⚡UTILITIES
TELEPHONE LOG

DATE	TIME	NAME	ADDRESS	REPAIR MAN	DIS. TIME	COMP. TIME
2/16	7:12p	B. ROPER	186 CHEW ST.	8	7:30p	7:50p
2/16	7:29p	G. MORRISI	S. POINT ST.	17	8:10p	8:55p
2/16	8:17p	K. SPENGLER	294 8TH ST.	15	8:30p	9:58p
2/16	8:42p	B. SEATED	26 BLAIR AVE.	8	9:30p	10:15p
2/16	9:35p	M. MUDD	15 SOUTH ST.	17	10:43p	12:36A
2/16	9:55p	R. LENON	7 W. POINT	9	10:55p	11:30p
2/16	10:30p	H. RUBIN	19 2ND AVE.	8	11:15p	11:35p
2/16	10:47p	D. CLARK	40 TOMS RD.	15	12:00A	12:20A

EXHIBIT C

VERDICT

MUDD KNEW
THE POWER HAD BEEN RESTORED.

EXHIBIT C shows the back room of Mudd's Diner after the supervisor arrived. An empty glass with ice cubes is on a table. If the electricity was out until shortly before the supervisor got there, it would have been impossible for Mudd to have used ice cubes in the drink. When Mudd realized he had ice, he knew the power had been restored the night before. This was confirmed when he replaced the burned-out light bulb. However, he had already turned away his lunchtime customers, so he said nothing to the supervisor so he could illegally sue the power company.

The Case of
The Speedy Jewel Thieves

LADIES AND GENTLEMEN OF THE JURY:
Whenever a theft occurs, a question logically arises. Did the person who was robbed fake the robbery in order to collect the insurance money?

That is the question presented to you today. Earl Rogers, the plaintiff, claims he was the victim of a robbery. Bowen Insurance Company, the defendant, refuses to pay the plaintiff's robbery claim. The insurance company's attorney states that there is not sufficient evidence to show that a robbery actually occurred.

Mr. Rogers has given the following testimony:

"On Sunday, June 20, at four o'clock in the afternoon, I was in my bedroom reading a book. The book was *Crime and Punishment*, to be exact. Deciding to take a nap, I lowered the shades and darkened the room. I was just drifting off to sleep when I heard strange noises coming from the den next to my bedroom."

Mr. Rogers put his ear to the bedroom door and strained to hear what was going on. From the sound, he knew that his den had been entered and a robbery was in progress. Mr. Rogers remained perfectly silent.

He could hear two voices. In the total darkness, he grabbed a pad and pencil and began to write down the conversation. For ten minutes, Mr. Rogers leaned against the door listening to the voices. Suddenly, all was quiet.

After a brief time, Mr. Rogers carefully opened the door and entered the den. A window was open. The robbers had used it to make good their escape. Mr. Rogers surveyed the room. All was in order except the bottom drawer of his desk, which had been locked. In it he kept a substantial amount of money and some jewelry. He found the drawer pulled open and completely empty.

Mr. Rogers estimates that $2,500 in cash and jewelry was stolen by the robbers. He would like the insurance company to pay him this amount so that he can replace his valuables.

After the robbery, the plaintiff immediately telephoned the police. EXHIBIT A is a photograph of the room taken shortly after the police arrived.

EXHIBIT B is the note written by Mr. Rogers as he listened at the door when the robbery was in progress. On it, he has written down some of the robbers' conversation. The names they called themselves are noted.

While the information Mr. Rogers had written down was scant, it provided police with sufficient details to search their files. The records of two criminals whose first names matched the ones Mr. Rogers had written down, and who were known accomplices are shown in EXHIBIT C.

Despite a search of their last known residence, police found no evidence that these men had been in the city at the time of the robbery.

Bowen Insurance company refuses to pay the $2,500 which Mr. Rogers has requested. The company insists there is weak evidence that a robbery took place. Instead, it charges that the plaintiff staged the theft. An investigator for the insurance company has explained to the court why his company refuses to pay the insurance claim. I quote from his statement:

"Mr. Rogers has reported two other robberies in the last three years. In each case there was no forcible entry. There were no clues to the theft, and the robberies remain unsolved.

"From the condition of the room following this present robbery, the police again found no evidence of forcible entry. You will note that the bottom drawer was not forcibly opened, despite the fact that Mr. Rogers has stated the drawer was always locked. This means that the robbers, if there truly were robbers, had to skillfully pick the lock to open the drawer.

"Since Mr. Rogers admits the robbers entered and left in a matter of ten minutes, we find his entire testimony highly suspect. Would intruders have entered the den without searching the rest of the house for valuables? Why did they limit themselves to the den? How did they know there were valuables in the bottom drawer? The relatively small amount stolen would not suggest a professional thief. We are asked to believe that two amateurs entered the house, picked the desk drawer lock, and escaped. All in a matter of ten minutes!

"In view of the plaintiff's previous reported thefts and the questions we raise about the present theft, my company refuses to pay the claim."

LADIES AND GENTLEMEN OF THE JURY: You have just heard the Case of the Speedy Jewel Thieves. You must decide the merit of Mr. Rogers' claim. Be sure to carefully examine the evidence in EXHIBITS A, B, and C.

Was a robbery committed? Or did Mr. Rogers stage the theft in order to collect the insurance money?

EXHIBIT A

Can you open the drawer?

Watch the lamp, Dave.

Hurry, I hear voices.

Look at this, Barry.

EXHIBIT C

RESIDENT KNOWN CRIMINAL

NAME Barry Waters

WHERE BORN USA

SEX M AGE 38 EYES Blue

HAIR Black HEIGHT 6'3" WEIGHT 216

DISTINCTIVE MARKS AND SCARS Scar above right eye

CRIMINAL SPECIALTY Breaking and entering

NAMES OF ASSOCIATES Dave Simpson

RESIDENT KNOWN CRIMINAL

NAME Dave Simpson

WHERE BORN USA

SEX M AGE 44 EYES Green

HAIR Brown HEIGHT 5'9" WEIGHT 150

DISTINCTIVE MARKS AND SCARS Missing finger, left hand

CRIMINAL SPECIALTY Breaking and entering

NAMES OF ASSOCIATES Barry Waters

VERDICT

THE ROBBERY WAS A FAKE.

Rogers said that he wrote down the conversation when his bedroom was in total darkness. But the words in EXHIBIT B are evenly spaced and are written in a straight line. Every *i* is precisely dotted and every *t* precisely crossed. This would have been impossible to do in a dark room.

Earl Rogers had faked the robbery.

The Case of
the Crazy Parrot

LADIES AND GENTLEMEN OF THE JURY:
When a store gives a warranty to its customers, the store must fully stand behind that warranty.

The case you are asked to decide today involves a pet shop. Mrs. Violet Hoffman, the plaintiff, says that the parrot she bought at King's Pet Shop has not lived up to the pet store's warranty. Mr. Tom King, the defendant, disagrees.

Mrs. Hoffman has given the following testimony:

"It was my son Billy's birthday. He's such a good boy, such an intelligent boy, such a creative and curious child, that I wanted to give him an unusual gift. I decided to buy him a pet parrot. I visited several shops before choosing what I thought was the perfect bird. My greatest concern was that I find a parrot that was well behaved."

Tom King, the owner of King's Pet Shop, assured Mrs. Hoffman he had exactly the bird she was looking for. He had trained the parrot himself. Mrs. Hoffman bought the parrot and gave it to her son on his birthday.

Billy named the parrot Long John Silver. Long John quickly became a member of the Hoffman family. It spoke out at the most unexpected times and became the center of attention.

One Saturday afternoon, Mrs. Hoffman returned home from the hairdresser. Billy met her at the door with a pained look on his face. When Mrs. Hoffman entered the house, she was horrified to find the living room in disarray. Sofa pillows were strewn on the floor. Books had toppled from the shelves. A large vase had fallen off a table and was lying cracked on the floor.

Long John Silver was sitting quietly, perched on his pedestal.

In tears, Billy told his mother that the parrot had gone berserk. Billy explained that while his mother had been gone, he had been doing his homework. He was typing a school paper when Long John Silver became excited, talking and squawking loudly.

As Billy finished his paper, Long John's squawking suddenly stopped. The parrot jumped off the perch and proceeded to fly wildly around the room. It spread its wings, knocking over everything in reach. When the parrot hit the vase, the crashing sound seemed to make it even crazier. It continued to fly around the room, grabbing pillows in its beak and dropping them as it flew from one place to another.

Billy finally caught the bird and managed to

fasten it to the perch.

Mrs. Hoffman claims that the parrot's behavior violates the pet store's warranty. She not only wants to return the bird but demands payment for the broken vase, which she says was worth $3,000.

EXHIBIT A is the store owner's warranty, found on the bill of sale.

EXHIBIT B is a photograph of the living room where the damage took place. You will note the entire room is in a state of disarray. Fortunately, the only permanent damage was to the vase.

Mr. Tom King, the pet store owner, represents himself as a professional animal trainer with fourteen years' experience. His sworn testimony states:

"I have personally trained hundreds of animals — including dozens of parrots. Remember the movie *The Purple Pirate?* I trained the parrots for all the pirates in that picture. No animal trained by me as a household pet has ever misbehaved in the manner claimed here today."

Mr. King feels strongly about his professional expertise and states the parrot could *not* have done the damage. He believes the damage was caused by someone else, perhaps Billy, and that Billy's story is a cover-up.

Mr. King's attorney has submitted EXHIBIT C as proof of this assertion. It is a blow-up of a section of the photograph in EXHIBIT B. It draws your attention to a boomerang that is lying on a shelf in the room. Mr. King believes the vase could have been easily knocked over by this toy. He states that such a toy does not belong in a living room.

Mr. King suggests that during Mrs. Hoffman's absence, Billy may have been playing with the boomerang and accidentally hit the vase. The other damage was done to cover up the accident and direct blame at the parrot.

Mr. King is willing to take back the parrot. But he flatly refuses to pay for the broken vase, as a matter of principle. His professional reputation has been challenged, and he does not believe that the parrot, which he personally trained, was the cause of the accident.

LADIES AND GENTLEMEN OF THE JURY: You have just heard the Case of the Crazy Parrot. You must decide the merit of Mrs. Hoffman's claim. Be sure to carefully examine the evidence in EXHIBITS A, B, and C.

Should King's Pet Shop pay for the damage? Or is someone else responsible for the damage, possibly Billy Hoffman?

EXHIBIT A

KING'S PET SHOP
TRAINING WARRANTY

King's Pet Shop warrants that birds trained by the store shall act in accordance with the behavior and in such manner as normally expected of birds who have undergone such training.

EXHIBIT B

EXHIBIT C

VERDICT

KING'S PET SHOP
DOES NOT HAVE TO PAY.

Billy claimed he was typing his school paper when the parrot became agitated. Exhibit B shows the living room with his paper in the typewriter.

The typewriter case is nearby. With the case in this position it would have been impossible to move the carriage backward and forward. Billy broke the vase and put the paper in the typewriter to pretend he was doing schoolwork.

The Case of
the Hunter's Shadow

LADIES AND GENTLEMEN OF THE JURY:
The difference between attempted murder and an accident may be as slight as the difference between breathing out and breathing in.

Please keep this in mind as you examine the case before you today. The State, represented by the district attorney, has accused John Goode of the attempted murder of Bradford Bedder. John Goode, the defendant, admits that he shot Bedder but says it was an accident.

John Goode has testified as follows:

"My name is John Goode. Two years ago, Bradford Bedder and I each invested $15,000 to build a sporting goods store on the outskirts of Walton City. The store's location is near a hunting preserve that attracts sportsmen from all over the county."

The men began with high hopes, calling the store Goode and Bedder Sporting Goods. On the day the store opened, each man bought the other a special hunting hat for good luck.

Despite good business when it opened, the store

soon ran into financial problems. A new discount store opened down the road and cut deeply into business. It sold the same kind of sports supplies as Goode and Bedder, but at much lower prices.

One day, John Goode decided to check the county files to see who owned the discount store. Much to his surprise, he found it was owned by his partner, Bradford Bedder. He concluded that Bedder was able to sell sports supplies for less at the discount store because the supplies had been secretly stolen from the Goode and Bedder warehouse.

John Goode was outraged! He immediately went to Bedder's home, only to learn that Bedder was camping with friends at the hunting preserve. Goode hurried to the campsite and saw Bedder standing outside a large tent.

Goode confronted Bedder with his findings and threatened him if he did not return the money he had made from the stolen supplies. Bedder simply laughed in his face, claiming that his partner could never prove he had stolen the supplies from the Goode and Bedder warehouse. John Goode, still angry, left the campsite.

Later that night, while Bradford Bedder was inside the tent playing cards with his friends, a rifle shot rang out. The shot pierced the side of the tent and Bedder fell down, a bullet lodged in his arm.

Gerald Pike, a fellow card player, darted outside

and ran after the intruder. He caught John Goode as he was running away, a rifle in his hand.

Police arrived and arrested Goode for the attempted murder of Bradford Bedder. But Goode claimed the shooting was an accident, and he had had no intention of harming Bedder. He said that he had decided their friendship was too important to lose over a business squabble, and he had decided to join the hunting party. As he was walking toward the front of the tent that night, the rifle fell out of his hand, hit the ground, and went off.

John Goode's attorneys have presented EXHIBIT A, which is a diagram of the tent where Bradford Bedder and his friends were playing cards when Bedder was shot. The spot is marked where John Goode was standing when he claimed he dropped his gun. Note that the tent flaps are closed, and there is no way Goode could have seen Bedder to purposely aim at him.

John Goode continues to claim that the shooting was an accident.

The district attorney called Gerald Pike to the witness stand. Mr. Pike testified that he had been in the tent earlier in the day and overheard John Goode threaten Bradford Bedder. EXHIBIT B presents Mr. Pike's testimony as he remembers the conversation. Goode was clearly angry and threatened Bedder, saying that if he did not pay back the money he stole, he would never live to spend it.

The district attorney has also presented EX-HIBIT C. He says it proves John Goode could have aimed at Bradford Bedder inside the tent even though the tent flaps were closed. He claims that Goode could have seen from the shadows on the outside wall of the tent, which man inside was his partner. Bedder and his friends were of similar height. But Goode could have identified Bedder if he somehow cast a shadow that was different than his friends.

The hats of Bedder and his two fellow hunters are shown in this exhibit. For demonstration purposes, the district attorney has placed a kerosene lantern similar to the one in the tent in front of the hats. A white background is behind them.

The district attorney has asked you to notice the similar shadows cast by two of the hats. But the shadow of the third hat, which is the special hunting hat Goode bought for Bedder, is very different. The district attorney has stated that Goode could easily have recognized the shadow of Bedder's hat, and he could have easily aimed at him and fired. Thus, the State claims, it *was* attempted murder.

LADIES AND GENTLEMEN OF THE JURY: You have just heard the Case of the Hunter's Shadow. You must decide the merits of the State's accusation. Be sure to carefully examine the evidence in EXHIBITS A, B, and C.

Was the shooting accidental? Or is John Goode guilty of attempted murder?

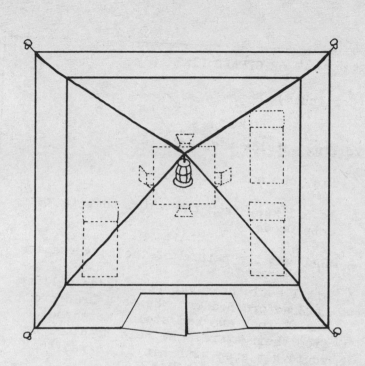

EXHIBIT B

STATEMENT OF GERALD PIKE

(Continued)

yelling outside the tent.

Q Did you look to see who it was?

A No. I knew from the voice that it was
John Goode.

Q What was the nature of the conversation?

A All I could hear was John Goode yelling
at Bradford Bedder. He said Bradford
was a crock and had stolen merchandise
from their store. He told Bradford he
would get even with him if it was the
last thing he ever did.

Q Did Goode threaten Bedder?

A Yes. He told Bradford to pay back the
money he had made on the stolen
supplies, or he would never live to
spend it.

EXHIBIT C

VERDICT

THE SHOOTING
WAS AN ACCIDENT.

In EXHIBIT A, the diagram of the tent, a kerosene lamp hanging from the ceiling is the only source of light. A light from above would have *cast all shadows on the floor*. From outside the tent, John Goode had no way of knowing where Bradford Bedder was sitting. Goode's story of the accidental firing was true.

YOU
BE
THE
JURY

Courtroom II

. . for Robby, again . . . .

Order in the Court

Ladies and Gentlemen of the Jury:

This court is now in session. My name is Judge John Dennenberg. You are the jury, and the trials are set to begin.

You have a serious responsibility. Will the innocent be sent to jail and the guilty go free? Let's hope not. Your job is to make sure that justice is served.

Read each case carefully. Study the evidence presented and then decide:

GUILTY OR NOT GUILTY??

Both sides of the case will be presented to you. The person who has the complaint is called the *plaintiff*. He or she has brought the case to court. If a crime is involved, the State is the accuser.

The person being accused is called the *defendant*. The defendant is pleading his or her innocence and presents a much different version of what happened.

IN EACH CASE, THREE PIECES OF EVIDENCE WILL BE PRESENTED AS

EXHIBITS A, B, AND C. EXAMINE THE
EXHIBITS VERY CAREFULLY. A *CLUE* TO
THE SOLUTION OF EACH CASE WILL BE
FOUND THERE. IT WILL DIRECTLY POINT
TO THE INNOCENCE OR GUILT OF THE
ACCUSED.

Remember, each side will try to convince you
that his or her version is what actually happened.
BUT YOU MUST MAKE THE FINAL DECI-
SION.

The Case of
the Flying Toy

LADIES AND GENTLEMEN OF THE JURY:

When a person invents something, that invention can be legally protected. The inventor fills out an application, and if the invention is found to be original, the United States Patent Office sends the inventor an official document called a patent. This prevents other people from using the inventor's idea.

The case you are asked to judge today involves a patented toy called SPIRALWIZ. This unusual flying toy has been sold worldwide by Backwards Industries, Incorporated.

Last year, Andrew Dobbs, who is the owner of a small plastics company, began selling an identical toy. He named it FLYFLIP.

Backwards Industries, the plaintiff, has asked the court to stop Andrew Dobbs from selling FLYFLIP because it is a copy of their invention. But Mr. Dobbs, the defendant, claims that his grandfather invented FLYFLIP 30 years ago, long before Backwards Industries had the idea.

A scientist for Backwards Industries has given the following testimony:

"My name is Dr. Robert Franklin. You might think that all scientists are nerdy people who walk around carrying test tubes and never have any fun, but at Backwards Industries we're not like that. In fact, my job is to sit around all day and think up ideas for new toys. I invented SPIRALWIZ for Backwards Industries.

"SPIRALWIZ is one of the most unusual floating toys ever invented. When you fling it in the air, it travels straight ahead. Then it rises skyward, flips upside down, and floats gently back into your hand."

EXHIBIT A is a photograph of this amazing toy.

As proof that SPIRALWIZ is an original invention, Backwards Industries also submitted EXHIBIT B. This is the patent issued to the scientist from Backwards Industries who claims to have invented SPIRALWIZ.

Andrew Dobbs challenges Backwards Industries. In claiming that the toy was an old idea of his grandfather's, he offers the following testimony:

"As a boy, I remember Gramps telling me about his idea for a toy that would fly back into the hands of the person who threw it. He was working on it for a long time. Then he surprised me one day when he brought home this fantastic gadget.

"We went out in the yard and he showed me how it worked. We took turns throwing the toy in the air. We played with it the whole afternoon. But Gramps had no idea of ever selling it as a product. He just worked on his ideas for the fun of it. In fact, the next day he was busy working on another invention, musical gum that plays a tune as you chew it."

While no one else saw Gramps' toy, Andrew Dobbs claims that his grandfather kept careful records. He had notebooks for all his inventions and they were stored in the attic when the old man died.

Mr. Dobbs located his grandfather's notes. EXHIBIT C is the last page of the notebook that shows a drawing of the toy. You will observe that the sketch is identical to SPIRALWIZ that Backwards Industries claims to have invented.

No one saw a working model of Gramps' toy besides Andrew Dobbs. But Mr. Dobbs offers the testimony of a friend who knew of his grandfather's experiments.

"My name is Charlie Watson. Gramps Dobbs was a good friend of mine. I know, I know. . . . You think it's funny that I called him Gramps when we weren't even related. But that's what everybody called him. I spent a lot of time with him when he was working on that crazy toy idea.

"Every day, for three weeks, I drove him to a remote field on the outskirts of town. Gramps didn't want anyone to see him working on his invention. To reach the field, we had to drive down a long, bumpy road that few people in town knew.

"I never bothered Gramps while he was trying to get the toy to work. I just went digging in the road, looking for unusual rocks for my geology collection. The road was covered with stones and rocks of all kinds. I used to find a lot of garnet and tourmaline.

"I clearly remember the last day we went to the field together. I was busy examining a large boulder when Gramps ran over to me very excited. He said he finally got his flying invention to work.

"But Gramps wouldn't show me the toy. He was very secretive about all his inventions.

"As we drove home, Gramps began writing in his notebook. He wouldn't even show me what he was writing. Then he slammed the notebook shut. He said, 'I'm glad that's finished. It took a long time to get that toy to work. Now on to my next invention.' "

"A lawyer for Backwards Industries claims the drawing in EXHIBIT C is a fake. He has stated:

"Except for the sketch on the last page, the notebook contains no written description of the invention — or statement that it even worked. There are no other drawings in the notebook.

"In fact, in this notebook, Grandfather Dobbs wrote about his experiments that failed. He never wrote that he could get the toy to work properly. And it seems strange that he would not show the invention to his friend, Charlie Watson. Could he have been ashamed that he had failed to get his toy to work?

"No, old Mr. Dobbs never got his flying toy to work. In fact, we believe his grandson Andrew Dobbs really drew the sketch himself. He knew he would have to stop selling FLYFLIP if Backwards Industries could prove to the court that the invention was theirs."

LADIES AND GENTLEMEN OF THE JURY:
You have just heard the Case of the Flying Toy. You must decide the merit of Backwards Industries' claim. Be sure to carefully examine EXHIBITS A, B, and C.

Was Grandfather Dobbs the original inventor of the flying toy? Or was the drawing in his notebook a fake?

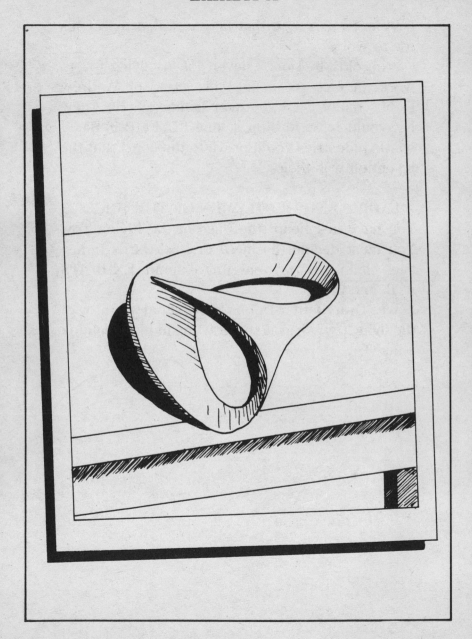

United States Patent Office

138,644
FLYING TOY
Robert Franklin, Freethrow, CA, assignor to
Backwards Industries, Inc., Freethrow, CA
Filed July 17, 1985, Ser. No. 21,655

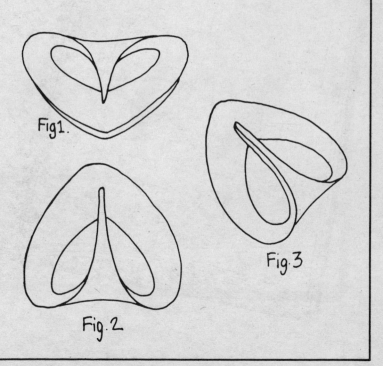

Fig1.

Fig. 2

Fig. 3

EXHIBIT C

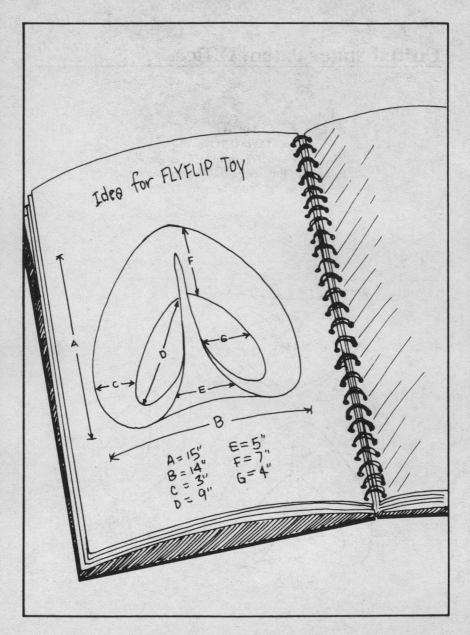

Idea for FLYFLIP Toy

A = 15"   E = 5"
B = 14"   F = 7"
C = 3"   G = 4"
D = 9"

VERDICT

THE DRAWING IN THE NOTEBOOK WAS A FAKE.

Charlie Watson testified that Grandpa Dobbs wrote the last page in his notebook while they were driving down a long, bumpy road. But the drawing and handwriting on the page are smooth and even, as though they had been written at a desk. Andrew Dobbs had added the final page himself.

The Case
of the Troublesome Twins

LADIES AND GENTLEMEN OF THE JURY:

For a person to be found guilty of a crime, there must be sufficient proof that he was the one who committed it.

Keep this in mind as you go over the facts of this very unusual case.

Farmer Foley, the plaintiff, accuses Bart Lee of breaking the lock on his chicken coop door. All the chickens escaped. He is suing Bart Lee for the amount of money it will take to replace the chickens.

Bart Lee, the defendant, claims he is not guilty of the crime since Farmer Foley cannot say for certain whether it was he or his twin brother who did it. If there is not enough evidence to point to either twin, then neither can be found guilty.

Farmer Foley has testified as follows:

"One rainy afternoon, April 19 to be exact, as I was sitting on the porch of my house, I saw a figure sneaking onto the far side of my property. The person was holding something that looked like a large stick.

"As I rose from my rocking chair, I saw the

intruder banging away at the chicken coop door. Seconds later, the vandal pulled the door open and the chickens rushed out, scurrying in all directions."

Farmer Foley chased the intruder through the muddy grounds. As he gained on him, the figure suddenly tripped and fell. When the person picked himself up, Foley grabbed him by the collar and marched him into the house.

The intruder turned out to be a young man of about nineteen years. He refused to identify himself. Despite the youth's pleas, Farmer Foley telephoned the police.

As they waited for the police to arrive, the intruder telephoned his brother and asked that he meet him at police headquarters.

When the police brought the intruder to the station, the young man was permitted to go into the next room to give his keys and money to his brother.

Minutes later, when the young man walked out of the room, the officer booked him for the crime. The youth said his name was Bart Lee, but he claimed he was innocent. And when his brother came out of the next room, he also claimed his innocence. To everyone's surprise, the brothers were identical twins!

While in the next room, the brothers had exchanged some of their clothing. They had purposely confused everyone.

I will now read from the testimony of the arresting officer. First the question and then his answer:

Q: How can you be sure that Bart Lee is the same twin you arrested?

A: Well, he was the first one out of the room. And he was wearing the same striped shirt as the guy I arrested at the farm.

Q: Was he wearing all the same clothing as the person you caught at the farm?

A: No. He had on some of his brother's clothes.

Q: What else was the person you arrested at the farm wearing?

A: I didn't notice everything. But he had on a dark jacket and dark-colored pants when I caught him.

Q: And what about the shirt he was wearing?

A: Yes, he had a striped shirt . I could see part of it under his jacket. And he had on sandals without socks.

The muddy ground around the chicken coop provided an important piece of evidence. This is shown in EXHIBIT A. Whoever broke into the coop left a trail of footprints behind.

EXHIBIT B is one of the sandals worn by the first twin to come out of the room . He identified himself as Bart Lee and is the twin who was booked for the crime. As you will note, an imprint of the sandal Bart was wearing exactly matches the footprints found around the chicken coop.

The arresting officer continued with his testimony as follows:

Q: What happened when you arrived with the vandal at police headquarters?

A: He asked my permission to go into the next room.

Q: Why did you let him?

A: Well, the kid seemed really scared. I figured his brother would quiet him down. But I didn't know that he had a *twin* brother in there.

Q: How long was he in the other room?

A: Only for a few minutes.

Q: Was it enough time for them to switch shirts, pants, and shoes?

A: I don't know.

EXHIBIT C is a photograph of both twins taken at the police station. One is wearing a light jacket and dark pants while the other has a dark jacket and light pants. Both have a shirt underneath. The twin on the left is Bart Lee, the one who was booked for the crime. He is wearing a striped shirt.

The lawyer for Farmer Foley raises an important question:

"Even though the brothers switched some of their clothing, why did the twin who was first to leave the room allow himself to be booked? That is, unless he really is the guilty one?

"Surely common sense argues that the twin who left the room first, and who is on trial here today, has to be the guilty party."

LADIES AND GENTLEMEN OF THE JURY:
You have just heard the Case of the Troublesome Twins. You are to decide the merit of Farmer Foley's accusation. Be sure to carefully examine the evidence in EXHIBITS A, B, C.

Was Bart Lee guilty of breaking open Farmer Foley's chicken coop? Or did his twin brother do it?

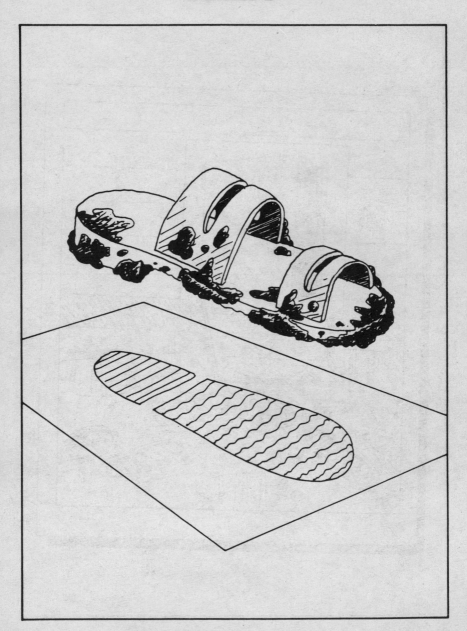

EXHIBIT C

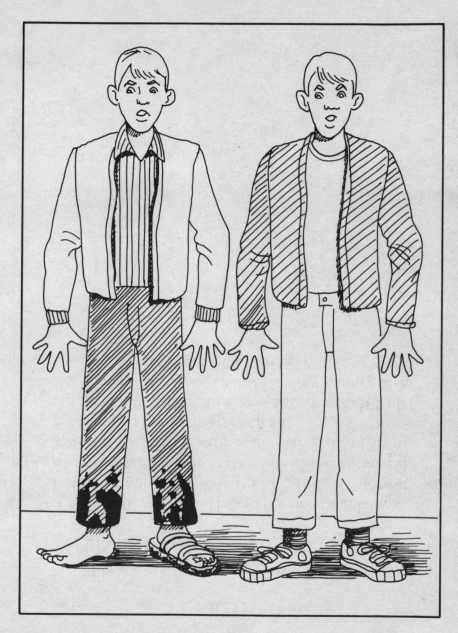

VERDICT

BART LEE WAS INNOCENT. HIS TWIN BROTHER WAS THE GUILTY ONE.

EXHIBIT B shows the mud-stained sandal that Bart wore at the police station. But the person wearing the sandals at the chicken coop would have his feet filthy with mud. Bart Lee's feet in EXHIBIT C are perfectly clean.

The clothing Bart Lee exchanged included his shoes and socks. His twin brother's muddy feet are inside Bart's socks and sneakers.

The Case of the Sleeping Prisoner

LADIES AND GENTLEMEN OF THE JURY:

Escape from jail is a serious crime, even if the person was arrested for a minor offense.

Such is the case before you today. Since we are in criminal court, the State is the accuser.

The State contends that Soney Najac, who was arrested for sleeping on a park bench, broke out of jail. But Mr. Najac claims his cell door was unlocked. He just pushed it open and walked out.

The patrolman, Thomas Nash, testifies as follows:

"It was about two o'clock in the morning and I was making my rounds in Vernon Park. No one is supposed to be there after dark.

"I was walking along when I heard a strange sound. At first I thought it might be thunder, but it was a starry night without any clouds. Then I realized what the sound was. Someone was snoring. I turned on my flashlight and there was this man on a bench. He was sound asleep.

"I tried to wake him but without success. I couldn't leave him there, so I figured the best thing to do was to strap him onto my motorcycle and drive down to police headquarters."

The stranger's wallet provided more information. His name was Soney Najac and the address inside showed he was from a foreign country.

The patrolman continued his testimony:

"The man was still asleep when I got to the station, so I carried him into a cell. It was my turn for night duty and I relieved the officer in charge.

"About six o'clock that morning, I went to the coffee shop around the corner to bring back some coffee and donuts. It couldn't have taken more than a few minutes.

"When I got back, I was shocked to find the cell door open. The prisoner had escaped."

All police were alerted. That afternoon Soney Najac was arrested in the downtown area, while he was looking in a store window. This time it was a more serious charge: escaping from jail.

The State described its theory of how Mr. Najac managed his escape. EXHIBIT A is a diagram showing the inside of the police station. It has two jail cells. On a side wall is a box containing keys. Mr. Najac was in the cell nearest the wall.

Two close-up photographs showing the key box are presented as EXHIBIT B. They show the box both open and closed. Each key is hanging on a large ring. If someone in a cell had a long pole, it would be possible for him to reach the key box.

This, the State contends, is how the breakout occurred. It enters as EXHIBIT C a photograph showing a broom that was found near Soney Najac's cell.

The State believes that the prisoner grabbed the broom, reached over to the box, and caught the key ring on one end. This was his means of escape.

I will now read for the cross-examination of Patrolman Nash by Mr. Najac's court-appointed lawyer:

Q: How can you be sure the cell door was locked?

A: I have been a policeman in this town for fifteen years. In all that time I never left a cell unlocked. What makes anyone think I did it this time?

Q: Did you find the door to the key box closed following the prisoner's departure?

A: It had to be. The door is on a spring and it swings closed automatically.

Q: Then how was it possible for Mr. Najac to use the broom to loop the key?

A: That's not hard to do. The ring on the front of the box can be pulled open with the broom handle. Then you can quickly catch the big key ring on the end of the broom before the door shuts. I know it can be done. I've tried it myself.

Soney Najac testified on his own behalf. Since

he could not speak English, his testimony was presented through an interpreter.

"My name is Soney Najac. I arrived in your country just two weeks ago. A friend told me I might find a good job in this area. So I took a bus to your town.

"I was tired from the trip and didn't have much money. When it got dark, I walked into the park and saw a bench. I hadn't had much sleep for the past few days, so I lay down on the bench for the night.

"When I woke up, I didn't know where I was. All I knew was that I was in this room with bars. No one else was around.

"I stood up and leaned against the door. It started to move, so I pushed it open and walked out. I never knew I had been arrested."

Mr. Najac's lawyer continues his defense:

"As proof that Mr. Najac did not use a key to escape from his cell, your attention is again drawn to EXHIBIT B. This photograph was taken shortly after the alleged breakout occurred.

"You will note the keys to both cells are hanging on their hooks. If Mr. Najac had used the key to escape, he never would have taken the time to put it back on its hook.

"The State's theory of the escape is hard to believe. The truth is simply this: Soney Najac woke up, didn't know where he was, found the cell door open — and just walked out!"

LADIES AND GENTLEMEN OF THE JURY:
You have just heard the Case of the Sleeping Prisoner. You must decide the merit of the State's accusation. Be sure to carefully examine the evidence in EXHIBITS A, B, and C.

Did Soney Najac escape from jail using a key? Or did he walk out of the unlocked door?

EXHIBIT A

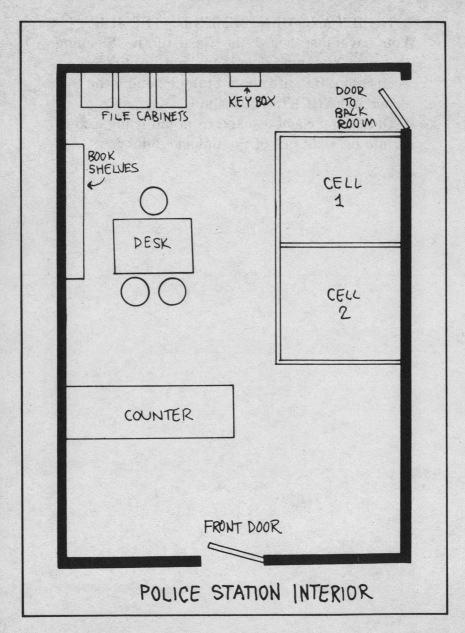

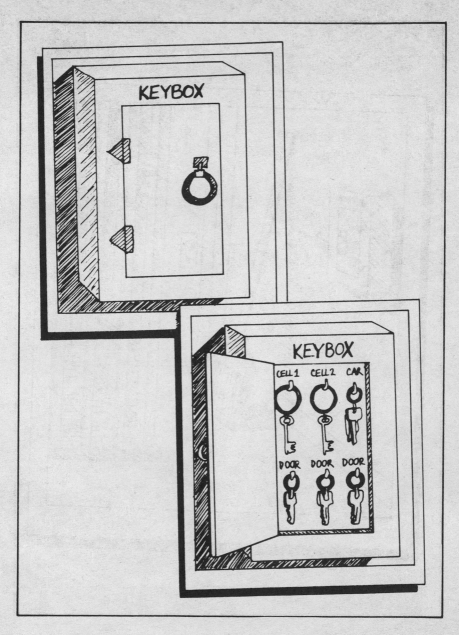

EXHIBIT C

VERDICT

THE CELL DOOR WAS NEVER LOCKED.

EXHIBIT B, on the left side, shows the key box as Soney Najac would have seen it when he awoke. Since he could not speak English, he could not have read the front of the box to know it contained the key to his cell.

The Case of
the High-Kicking Horse

LADIES AND GENTLEMEN OF THE JURY:

If a horse owner does not properly train his horse and it injures someone, the owner is responsible.

Tom Clive, the plaintiff, allegedly was kicked in the head by a horse called Lightning. He suffered severe head injuries and is suing Howard Simm, the owner. He claims that if Lightning had been properly trained, the horse would not have kicked him. Howard Simm, the defendant, says that the horse was well trained.

Tom Clive has testified as follows:

"My name is Tom Clive. I'm a successful jockey who's worked for a number of the top horse owners in the country. I'm the best and I don't care who knows it. Maybe you saw me last year in the Kentucky Derby. Anyway, I was hired by Howard Simm to ride his horse Lightning in the Langdon Races.

"But the first day I was working out with Lightning, Mr. Simm walked up to me and fired me. Just like that! For no reason at all. He told me to get off his property and he'd send me my riding gear the next day.

"Well, I was so angry with Howard Simm that I decided I wasn't going to wait until the next day for my things. I wanted to clear out that night and never see the owner again.

"I snuck back to the stable around midnight. The light in the stable must have been out, so I felt my way to the rear of the stable and over to my locker. I grabbed my gear and headed for the door. Then I remembered I'd left my riding crop inside Lightning's stall.

"When I went to get my riding crop, Lightning was restless and neighing. As I opened the stall door, the horse reared its hind legs and began kicking. He caught me on my forehead. My head still hurts when I think about it.

"I must have been out for hours. When I awoke it was dawn. I could see that Lightning was inside his stall."

Thomas Clive's lawyer entered as EXHIBIT A a photograph of the stall as it appeared that morning.

He also entered as EXHIBIT B a photograph of the baseball hat Thomas Clive was wearing at the time he suffered the injury. Mr. Clive says the horseshoe mark on the hat shows where Lightning kicked him.

In his testimony, Howard Simm raised doubt about Clive's account of the accident. First the question and then his answer:

Q: Why do you question the facts of Tom Clive's story?

A: Well, I didn't like Clive's attitude from the start. I knew he had had trouble with other owners, but I decided to hire him anyway.

Q: What made you change your mind?

A: It was after Clive had his first workout with Lightning. He said my horse wasn't well trained. He called Lightning too wild to be a winner.

Q: Is that when you fired Mr. Clive?

A: Sure. I didn't want a person like him riding Lightning. So I told the jockey he was finished.

Q: What was his reaction?

A: He never expected me to fire him. When I told him I would get another jockey instead, Clive became very angry. He said I would regret it.

Howard Simm offered another explanation for the jockey's injury:

"I don't know why Tom Clive decided to pick up his riding things that night. I told him I'd send them the next day. He might have been trying to hurt Lightning.

"I can't say whether Lightning kicked the jockey or not. But if Clive was stupid enough to go into my stable after dark, he should have known it might be dangerous. Clive could have banged his head on anything. He would have had trouble walking through the stable in the dark."

He entered EXHIBIT C, a photograph of Tom Clive's locker, to prove his theory.

"Clive could easily have hit his head on that beam near his locker and used the accident to blame Lightning. He said he would get even with me. Maybe he even faked the whole thing.

"There are old horseshoes inside the barn. If Clive wanted to blame Lightning, all he had to do was find one and slam it into his baseball hat.

"You can't tell from the mark on Tom Clive's hat whether it was done by Lightning or not. Any old horseshoe could have done it."

LADIES AND GENTLEMEN OF THE JURY:
You have just heard the Case of the High-Kicking Horse. You must decide the merit of Tom Clive's claim. Be sure to carefully examine the evidence in EXHIBITS A, B, and C.

Did Lightning kick Tom Clive? Or did the jockey fake the accident?

EXHIBIT A

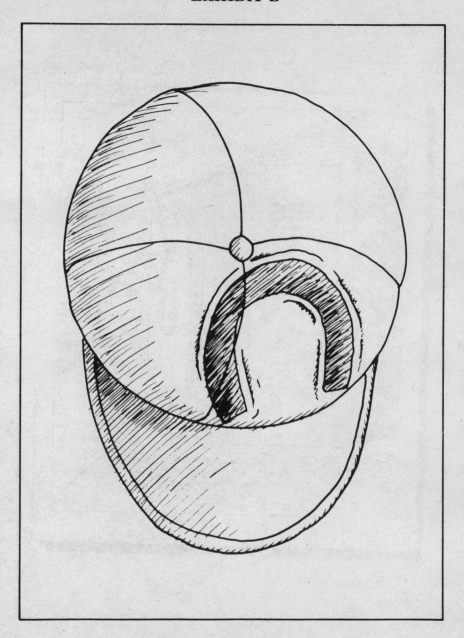

EXHIBIT C

VERDICT

TOM CLIVE FAKED THE HORSESHOE MARK ON HIS HAT.

The mark in EXHIBIT B shows the horseshoe had hit the hat with a downward blow. Clive overlooked the fact that horses kick *upward*. If Lightning had kicked him, the horseshoe mark would have been turned upside down with the round part on the bottom.

The Case of
the Leaky Basement

LADIES AND GENTLEMEN OF THE JURY:

When an agreement is made in writing, it becomes a legal obligation.

This is the point of law you must keep in mind today.

George Clark, the plaintiff, agreed to buy a house from Lester Lyon for $94,000. Mr. Clark then wrote a letter to Lester Lyon confirming their agreement. He enclosed a $1,000 check as a deposit.

But Mr. Clark discovered the house was poorly built and withdrew his offer. He is suing Lester Lyon, the defendant, because Mr. Lyon won't return his deposit.

George Clark has testified as follows:

"When I first looked over Mr. Lyon's house, it seemed just what I wanted. I liked the layout and its location. I agreed to his selling price provided the house was inspected by a professional construction engineer. I didn't want any surprises after I bought it.

"Mr. Lyon told me he had others who wanted to purchase his house. He said that if I were serious about my offer, I should confirm it in writing and enclose a $1,000 deposit.

"I agreed, and sent him a letter the next day.

EXHIBIT A is the check George Clark sent to Mr. Lyon.

Mr. Clark hired a construction engineer to inspect the house. When the engineer brought the report to Mr. Clark's home, it was unsatisfactory. It seems Lyon's house was built on land that was once a swamp. A heavy rain could cause basement flooding. A real storm might even make the house float away. The engineer showed Mr. Clark a picture he had taken of watermarks in the basement.

When the engineer showed him the photograph, George Clark immediately telephoned the owner. He told Lyon their deal was off and requested that he return the $1,000.

"When I told Lester Lyon I was withdrawing my offer, he warned me that if I did, I wouldn't get back my deposit. And he told me I had agreed the money was his no matter what happened. He said I wrote that in the letter I sent him.

"I couldn't believe it. I certainly never wrote any such thing. I pulled out my checkbook to show the engineer that Lyon must have been mistaken. On the stub of the check I had written a note to myself that it was a 'refundable deposit.'

"The engineer took out his camera and photographed my checkbook. He said it would be important evidence if I ever had to go to court."

This photograph was entered as EXHIBIT B. The engineer has sworn under oath that he was with George during the telephone conversation.

Lester Lyon had a very different story to tell:

"When I put a notice in the newspaper advertising my house for sale, four people called to say they were interested. I decided to sell my house to Clark because he was the first to come over.

"When Mr. Clark and I agreed on the purchase price, I told him about the other people interested in buying it. I accepted his bid only when he agreed to send me the deposit. He knew he wouldn't get it back if he withdrew his offer."

George Clark's letter accompanying the check appears as EXHIBIT C. It proves that Mr. Clark's purchase of the house depended on the inspection by a professional engineer.

Mr. Lyon's attorney has called your attention to the note at the bottom of this letter. It clearly states that George Clark agreed that the deposit was not refundable.

Mr. Clark claims he wrote the top part of the letter in EXHIBIT C, but not the wording at the bottom. He accuses Lester Lyon of introducing false evidence into court. He claims Mr. Lyon added the bottom section after he received George Clark's letter.

Lester Lyon was able to get another buyer for his house. It was sold at the same price as George

Clark's offer. But he refuses to return the $1,000.

LADIES AND GENTLEMEN OF THE JURY:
You have just heard the Case of the Leaky Basement. You must decide the merit of George Clark's claim. Be sure to carefully examine the evidence in EXHIBITS A, B, and C.

Can Lester Lyon keep the $1,000 deposit? Or did he add the wording to George Clark's letter?

GEORGE CLARK
505 BENNET DR.
HANOVER, NC. 10321

1426

October 12, 19 88

Pay to the
order of   Lester Lyon $ 1000 xx

One thousand and xx/100 ~~~~~~~~~~~~~~~~~~~~ Dollars

RIGIDITY
BANK

For   Deposit   George Clark

02170032

EXHIBIT B

EXHIBIT C

GEORGE CLARK

October 12, 1988

Mr. Lester Lyon
857 Front St.
Hanover, N.C.

Dear Mr. Lyon:

Confirming our meeting yesterday, I wish to acknowledge my interest in purchasing your house for $94,000.00. This purchase is subject to satisfactory inspection by a professional builder.

As you requested, enclosed is a check for $1,000.00 as a deposit.

Sincerely,

George Clark

PS. **I understand that the $1,000.00 deposit is not refundable to me.**

VERDICT

LESTER LYON TYPED THE BOTTOM OF THE LETTER.

The bottom sentence of the letter in EXHIBIT C contains asterisks. But the photograph in exhibit B shows that George Clark's typewriter does not have an asterisk key. It could not have been typed on Clark's typewriter.

The Case of
the Missing Ring

LADIES AND GENTLEMEN OF THE JURY:

Grand larceny is a very serious crime. It is the theft of something worth a great deal of money.

Dora Watson, the plaintiff, has accused Fritz Lindsay of breaking into her bedroom and stealing her expensive diamond ring. Fritz Lindsay, the defendant, states that the ring was never stolen. He claims it was lost by Mrs. Watson. He found it in a movie theater the same evening she was there.

Mrs. Watson has testified as follows:

"On Saturday evening, July 8, my husband and I went out to see a movie. Our daughter Jennifer was baby-sitting for our three-year-old son.

"When we returned home late that evening, I realized the ring was not on my finger. But I thought I had just forgotten to put it on when I dressed for the theater. I searched frantically in our bedroom, but I couldn't find the ring anywhere.

"When I couldn't find the ring at home, I figured I must have worn it to the theater and it had fallen off my finger that evening. It had been a little loose and I had meant to get it tightened. I called Blake

Theater to see if anyone had found a ring. But no one had reported it."

Mrs. Watson's daughter stated that while she was baby-sitting the evening her parents went out, she heard a strange noise in their bedroom. When she went upstairs to check, nothing seemed wrong. But as she looked out the bedroom window, she saw a man walking across the lawn of their house. Jennifer didn't think much of it until her mother said the ring was missing.

Mrs. Watson placed an ad in the paper offering a reward to anyone finding her diamond ring. This advertisement is entered as EXHIBIT A.

The day the ad appeared, Fritz Lindsay came to the Watson house. He explained to Mrs. Watson that he had been in the Blake Theater the same evening that she was. He was one of the last to leave and had found a ring on the floor in a corner of the lobby.

Fritz Lindsay removed a diamond ring from his pocket and asked Mrs. Watson if she could identify it. Mrs. Watson was thrilled. Her ring had been found. She gladly offered to pay Lindsay the reward money.

This diamond ring is entered as EXHIBIT B.

During all the excitement, Jennifer whispered to her father that Fritz Lindsay looked just like the man she had seen walking across the lawn that Saturday evening. Mr. Watson slipped into the kitchen and called the police.

While Fritz Lindsay was still at the Watson home, the police arrived. They arrested him for the theft of Mrs. Watson's diamond ring. He is charged here today with grand larceny.

The lawyer for the defense claimed that the identification of Fritz Lindsay was a case of mistaken identity. At the time Jennifer looked out the bedroom window, it was very late at night. It would have been difficult to see clearly the person who was in her backyard.

Fritz Lindsay testified as follows:

"I was nowhere near the Watson house that night. When I saw the ad in the paper, I thought it might be talking about the ring I found. I was only trying to do a good deed."

Mr. Lindsay provided proof that he was at the theater the same night as Mr. and Mrs. Watson. While he could not produce a witness who saw him, he entered as evidence a torn ticket stub from the movie. This is shown in EXHIBIT C.

The management of Blake Theater acknowledged that the stub was from a ticket purchased on the same Saturday the Watsons went to the theater. But they were unable to verify the exact time it was bought.

Fritz Lindsay continued his testimony:

"When the movie was over I stopped at a vending machine to buy some candy. As I was eating it, I saw something shiny in the corner. To my surprise, I discovered it was an expensive ring. The manager of the theater wasn't around and I didn't want to leave it with anyone else. So I took the ring home.

"I never stole any ring. I found it in the theater and that reward money is mine."

LADIES AND GENTLEMEN OF THE JURY:
You have just heard the Case of the Missing Ring. You must decide the merits of Dora Watson's accusation. Be sure to carefully examine the evidence in EXHIBITS A, B, and C.

Did Fritz Lindsay steal Mrs. Watson's ring? Or did he find it at the Blake Theater?

ANNOUNCEMENTS

ATTENTION DIETERS
Try new Tropical Treat diet. All
you eat is pineapple. Saves
you money. Call 505-3000.

LOST BANK BOOK
01-342-7-5020
If found please return to
H. Hughes, Las Vegas, Nevada.

REWARD
For return of diamond ring lost
in or near Blake Theater
on July 8.
Contact: P.O. Box 352
Harmony, N.Y. 17834

PUPPET SHOWS
Lifelike entertainment for
parties. These puppets look so
real . . . maybe they are!
Call M. Giappetto, 355-1212.

EXHIBIT B

EXHIBIT C

VERDICT

FRITZ LINDSAY STOLE THE RING.

The ad in EXHIBIT A contains a post office box number, not Mrs. Watson's address. Lindsay could not have known where the owner of the ring lived unless he had stolen it from her house.

The Case of
the Broken Display Case

LADIES AND GENTLEMEN OF THE JURY:

When a person on trial for a crime cannot be positively identified, then the court may rely on circumstantial evidence. Circumstantial evidence is a group of facts that can lead the jury to decide if a person is guilty or innocent. There must be enough evidence to prove a person guilty beyond a shadow of a doubt.

The State has accused Edward Carlson, the defendant, of breaking the glass display case in the Sheridan School gym with the intent to steal a valuable trophy. Mr. Carlson claims he is innocent of the crime.

The State called Steven Stone, the Sheridan School principal, to the witness stand:

"Every year during spring vacation, Sheridan School holds its annual fair. This year the money we raised was used to buy new equipment for the soccer team.

"The fair is a major event. Everyone in the community looks forward to it. There are booths with games of chance and skill. Other booths have food and student crafts for sale.

"The fair is held in the school gym. This year Edward Carlson, a cafeteria worker, volunteered to be in charge of the bowling booth.

"At six o'clock on the evening before the fair, I was about to leave the school for the night. As I passed the gym, I heard a strange noise inside. When I opened the door I could see someone at the far end of the gym, standing over the display case. He was holding a large object raised over his head.

"Before I could yell for him to stop, he smashed the top of the display case with the object."

EXHIBIT A is a photograph of the broken display case. The sterling silver trophy inside was untouched. The principal had interrupted the intruder before he was able to remove it.

The principal continued his testimony:

"I chased the intruder and he ran into the boys' locker room. I was right behind him. From the locker room he ran into the gym office and then out a rear door. He was running too fast for me to catch him."

The principal was unable to see the face of the intruder, but he described him as a male, approximately six feet tall and wearing a white T-shirt, dark pants, and sneakers.

When the principal returned to the gym office,

he noticed a bowling pin lying on the floor. It looked like the object used to break the display case. It was turned over to police and examined for fingerprints.

The pin, with its print marks, is entered as EXHIBIT B. Because the bowling pin was scratched from use, it is impossible to tell for sure if it was the object used to smash the display case.

The police determined the prints on the bowling pin match those of Edward Carlson. Further investigation has shown the defendant has a criminal record of petty larceny (or small thefts). A record of his arrest and his fingerprint file are shown as EXHIBIT C.

The testimony of Edward Carlson was then presented. First the question and then his answer:

Q: Where were you at six o'clock on the evening before the fair?

A: I finished setting up the bowling booth and left school around four o'clock. At six o'clock I was in my apartment watching television.

Q: Was there anyone with you who can verify that you were in your apartment at the time in question?

A: I live alone with my dog, Mutt. I don't remember anyone seeing me enter that night.

Q: Does that mean you have no one who can verify your whereabouts at six o'clock?

A: No one saw me.

144

Q: How do you account for your fingerprints on the bowling pin?

A: Sure they are my prints. I picked up a bunch of bowling pins from the supply closet in the gym office. They were for the fair booth. I made two trips to the office. One was for the bowling balls and the other for the pins.

Q: But why was the bowling pin in EXHIBIT B found on the gym office floor?

A: My arms were full. I must have dropped one while I was carrying them to the gym.

Q: If you dropped a bowling pin, why didn't you pick it up?

A: I never actually heard a pin fall. But one must have dropped. That's the only way I can explain it being on the office floor. There was banging and sawing going on in the gym. Other people were setting up their booths. There was too much noise to hear a bowling pin drop.

The defense claims that since the principal never saw the intruder drop a bowling pin as he chased him, there is no way to prove the pin on the office floor was the object used to break the display case.

The State claims that since the bowling pin found on the office floor bears the fingerprints of Edward Carlson, then it is logical to conclude that he was the intruder and that he dropped the pin as he was chased by the principal.

LADIES AND GENTLEMEN OF THE JURY:
You have just heard the Case of the Broken Display Case. You must decide the merits of the State's claim. Be sure to carefully examine the evidence in EXHIBITS A, B, and C.

Was Edward Carlson the person who smashed the display case? Or was the intruder someone else?

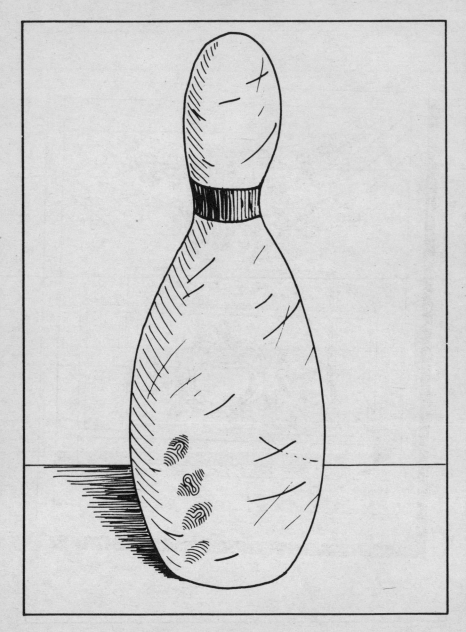

EXHIBIT C

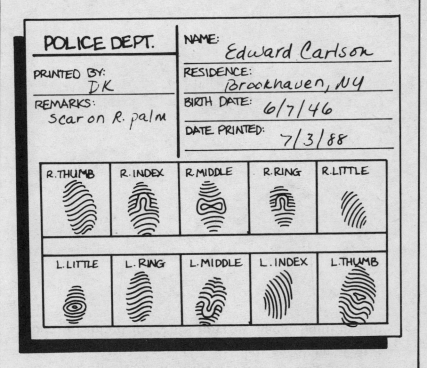

POLICE DEPT.

PRINTED BY: DK

REMARKS: Scar on R. palm

NAME: Edward Carlson

RESIDENCE: Brookhaven, NY

BIRTH DATE: 6/7/46

DATE PRINTED: 7/3/88

R. THUMB	R. INDEX	R. MIDDLE	R. RING	R. LITTLE

L. LITTLE	L. RING	L. MIDDLE	L. INDEX	L. THUMB

VERDICT

EDWARD CARLSON WAS NOT GUILTY.

The fingerprints in EXHIBIT B show how Carlson had grabbed the bowling pin. He held the wide part of the pin. If the bowling pin had been used to smash the display case, he would have grabbed it by its narrow neck, holding the pin upside down.

The Case of
the Mysterious Fire

LADIES AND GENTLEMEN OF THE JURY:

When a fire occurs, a question logically arises. Was the fire accidental or was it started on purpose, perhaps to collect insurance money?

That is the question presented to you today. Brenda Taylor, the plaintiff, seeks to collect insurance because her jewelry store was badly damaged by fire. Rightup Insurance Company refuses to pay the claim. The insurance company believes there is sufficient evidence to prove the fire was started on purpose.

Ms. Taylor is the owner of Jewelry Gems. The store had been in business for eight years. She gave the following testimony:

"I arrived at my store at the usual time, around 8:30 in the morning. As I put my key in the lock I could smell something burning. I opened the door and a burst of smoke hit me in the face.

"I screamed for help. Flames were creeping down from the ceiling. The smoke was so thick, I could barely see across the room.

"I hurried to save what I could. I emptied out a

drawer and began filling it with all the expensive jewelry I could find. But the smoke was too much. I could hardly breathe. That's when I ran outside. Just then, the fire truck arrived."

The fire captain said his station had received a phone call from an upstairs neighbor at 8:25 A.M. He met Brenda Taylor as she was running out of the store. She was gasping for breath.

As he took the drawer from her arms she collapsed on the sidewalk. The captain comforted Ms. Taylor while the men went inside.

A half hour later the fire was under control. But the damage was already done. The fire had been burning for hours. The display cases and shelves were badly damaged.

It was determined that weeks before the fire, Brenda Taylor had remodeled her store, purchased new display cases and more jewelry and installed a new lighting system. On the basis of its inspection, the fire department believes the fire broke out in the ceiling. But fire inspectors were unable to determine if defective wiring was the cause.

EXHIBIT A is the fire department report. It describes the heavy damage done by the fire.

EXHIBIT B is a photograph taken outside of the store minutes after the fire truck arrived. Thick smoke was still pouring out of the front of the jewelry store.

An investigator for the insurance company has explained to the court why his company refuses to pay the insurance claim. I quote from his statement:

"About two weeks before the fire, Brenda Taylor took out additional insurance with my company. She increased the amount by $30,000. We have determined that this amount was not justified by her remodeling costs or the additional things she purchased."

Rightup Insurance has entered as EXHIBIT C the new insurance policy.

The insurance investigator had looked into the financial affairs of Ms. Taylor and continued his testimony.

"My investigation shows that Ms. Taylor's business had fallen off about six months ago when a discount jewelry store opened down the street. In recent months, she twice missed payment of her rent.

"She told the landlord she could not afford to pay because business was so bad. According to the landlord, Brenda Taylor tried to break her rental lease, claiming the discount store was forcing her out of business.

"We further learned that Ms. Taylor had a meeting with a real estate agent in the next town. She told him she was interested in space to open a new store.

"We find it suspicious that Ms. Taylor would remodel her store while looking for a different location at the same time. We believe she did the remodeling as an excuse to increase the amount of her fire insurance.

"We find Brenda Taylor's actions highly questionable. It is our belief that Ms. Taylor was responsible for the fire in her jewelry store. She needed the insurance money to pay her debts.

"The fire also was a convenient excuse to move to a new location. Otherwise, why would she have been looking for a new store?

"In view of the excessive amount of Brenda Taylor's new insurance policy and her suspicious activities in the weeks prior to the fire, my company refuses to pay the claim."

LADIES AND GENTLEMEN OF THE JURY:
You have just heard the Case of the Mysterious Fire. You must decide the merits of Brenda Taylor's claim. Be sure to carefully examine the evidence in EXHIBITS A, B, and C.

Did the fire break out accidentally? Or did Brenda Taylor start it?

EXHIBIT A

REPORT OF FIRE IN A BUILDING

Time of alarm __8:25 AM__   Date __JULY 3, 1987__

Discovered by __CARL FRANKS__

Building where fire started __JEWELRY GEMS__

__FIRST FLOOR AT 635 WALKER STREET__

Height (stories) __3__   Construction __BRICK__

Walls __BRICK__   Floor __WOOD__   Roof __PROTECTED__

Cause __UNKNOWN. POSSIBLY DEFECTIVE WIRING__

__IN CEILING__

Date property last inspected __JUNE 27, 1987__

Loss of life or injuries __NONE —__

__CONSIDERABLE DAMAGE TO CEILING AND__

__SHELVES, FURNITURE, ETC. SMOKE__

__DAMAGE TO WALLS.__

EXHIBIT C

EXHIBIT C

COMMERCIAL PROPERTY COVERAGE
DECLARATION PAGE

POLICY NO. 57216 EFFECTIVE DATE 6/16/87

NAME INSURED

Brenda Taylor
Jewelry Gems
635 Walker St. Flanders, Wisc.

DESCRIPTION OF PREMISES

First floor of brick, three-story bldg.

COVERAGE PROVIDED

PREM NO.	BLDG. NO.	COVERAGE	LIMIT OF INS.	COVERED CAUSES	CO-INS.	RATES
136	2	contents	$110,000	fire		$2,200
		improvements	25,000	fire		500
						$2,700

DEDUCTIBLE

NONE

VERDICT

THE FIRE WAS SET BY BRENDA TAYLOR.

EXHIBIT B shows the jewelry Brenda Taylor had thrown into the drawer before she ran out of the burning store. The boxes were neatly stacked, with the smaller ones on top of the larger ones. If she had hurried to fill it, the boxes would have been scattered in the drawer in no special order.

Taylor packed the drawer with the jewelry *before* she set fire to the store. She left and returned to save the valuables when the fire began to rage.

The Case of
the Polluted River

LADIES AND GENTLEMEN OF THE JURY:

Pollution of the environment is a crime our society cannot allow. It endangers the quality of life both today and for future generations.

The State has accused Chemzon Industries of unlawfully dumping toxic waste in the waters of the Rhonda River. Chemzon Industries claims that it disposes of waste at its own safe dumping site and that the State's charges are unfounded.

The State called as its first witness Billy Lang, one of two boys who were floating on their raft down the Rhonda River.

"My friend and I had just built the raft. We thought it would be fun to have summer camping trips along the banks of the Rhonda.

"The day after school was over, we took our first trip. We set sail from the dock at Cedar Park. My friend was sunning himself and I was the navigator.

"We were drifting along for about fifteen minutes. I was looking into the water to see how far down I could see. All of a sudden I saw a dead fish float by our raft. As we drifted downstream, I spotted another dead fish and then another. Before I knew it, I saw pockets of them surfacing all around the raft.

"I grabbed one of the fish and pushed the raft toward shore. I thought the police should know what I found.

"As I neared shore, I saw this empty barrel floating in the water. My friend helped me pull it onto the raft."

EXHIBIT A is the cardboard barrel found by Billy Lang. The label clearly shows it contains Zendrite, a hazardous chemical. Markings on the barrel prove it is the property of Chemzon Industries.

Chemzon is a company that makes insecticides. The poisonous chemical, Zendrite, is a waste product that is left over after the insecticides have been made.

State law says that toxic chemical waste may not be dumped in any rivers. The law requires companies to get rid of their waste at special disposal sites.

The law was passed because companies were using the Rhonda River for dumping waste. Local fishermen complained that fishing conditions in the river had slowly become worse over the years. Before the law was passed, companies would drive trucks to an inlet along the river. They would empty barrels of chemicals into its waters. The barrel found by Billy Lang was floating near the river's inlet.

EXHIBIT B is a map of part of the Rhonda River. The location where Billy discovered the barrel is marked with an X.

Fred Chesterton, a vice president of Chemzon, was called to testify. First the question and then his answer:

Q: Has your company ever dumped chemicals into the Rhonda River?

A: Yes. We used to do it by the inlet like everyone else. There was a road leading to the water. That was before the State passed the new law. Now we take waste to our own disposal site.

Q: How often do you do this?

A: About every two weeks. Our own site is just outside of town.

EXHIBIT C is a photograph of the Chemzon waste site.

Q: Isn't it true that your waste site is nearly filled and your company has been trying to find land for a new one?

A: Yes. But we can still use our site for several months before it's full.

Q: How do you account for the barrel found in the Rhonda River?

161

A: I don't really know. It could have been an accident. Maybe when our truck was taking the waste from our plant to our dumping site, one of the barrels accidentally fell off the truck and rolled into the river. It could have floated to the inlet. Our loading dock is at the rear of the plant near the river.

Q: But the top of the barrel was missing. Aren't the barrels closed before they are loaded on your truck?

A: Yes they are. But it wouldn't take much for the top to fall off. We reuse the barrels and the tops don't always fit tightly.

The State feels that the death of the fish in the Rhonda River was not caused by a single barrel of chemicals. Rather, it was the result of frequent use of the river as a dumping ground. The State accuses Chemzon Industries of regularly dumping Zendrite into the water because their waste site was nearly full.

The State claims that while someone from Chemzon was pouring the toxic chemicals into the water by the inlet, the barrel accidentally fell into the river. It accuses Chemzon Industries of willfully violating the pollution law.

LADIES AND GENTLEMEN OF THE JURY:
You have just heard the Case of the Polluted River. You must decide the merit of the State's accusation.

Be sure to carefully examine the evidence in EXHIBITS A, B, and C.

Did Chemzon Industries purposely dump toxic waste into the Rhonda River? Or did the barrel accidentally fall off a truck at its plant?

EXHIBIT A

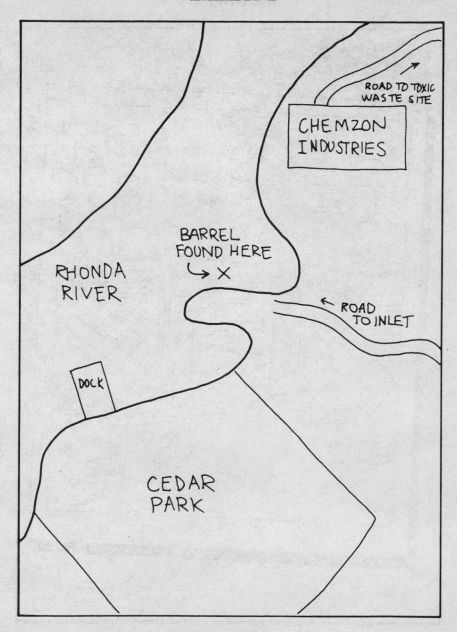

EXHIBIT C

VERDICT

CHEMZON INDUSTRIES IS GUILTY OF POLLUTION.

Billy Lang's raft was drifting downstream from the dock in Cedar Park, so the river was flowing in the direction *toward* Chemzon's plant. If the barrel had accidentally fallen off a truck at Chemzon's plant, it would have floated downstream, in the direction *away from* the inlet.

Instead, the barrel was found floating near the inlet. It had fallen into the water at that location.

The Case of
the Broken Goldfish Bowl

LADIES AND GENTLEMEN OF THE JURY:

A person who is found at the scene of a crime is not necessarily a criminal.

Keep this in mind as you decide the case before you today.

The crime presented here today may seem unusual. No money or property was stolen. Rather, the act was one of outright vandalism in which someone purposely wrecked the rear room of the Pets-R-People Pet Shop.

James Bradley, the owner of the Pets-R-People Pet Shop, has accused Mike Webster of purposely wrecking the back room of the store. Mike Webster, a former employee of the store, claims he is innocent.

A night watchman has given the following testimony:

"It was on the night of August 17 that I was making my rounds at Concord Mall when I heard strange noises coming from the Pets-R-People Pet Shop. I tried the front door and found it unlocked. After contacting the owner, I entered the store.

"Nothing seemed unusual. I made my way to the rear. As I pulled apart the curtains leading to the back room, I was startled to find Mike Webster sprawled facedown on the floor.

"The rear room was a mess. Papers, bills, and files were torn and scattered throughout the room. Boxes were opened, their contents littered about. Piles of spilled pet food were all over the floor."

The watchman shook Webster and the man stirred. Half dazed, he rose to his feet.

Webster said he had gone to the pet store after it had closed because he had forgotten to feed the goldfish. While he was there, he heard the front door open. He called out, thinking it was the owner. Suddenly, he was rushed by a young teenage boy. Webster had never seen him before.

Webster was so frightened that he fainted, falling on the floor. This was the last he remembered until he was awakened by the night watchman. The police were called and they arrested Mike Webster.

James Bradley, the owner of Pets-R-People, testified as follows:

"Hey, I'm a nice guy, but Mike Webster was a terrible clerk. He often arrived late and spent time in the back room when he should have been helping customers.

"I finally had to talk to him about his poor performance. To my surprise, he started yelling and screaming at me that he worked as hard as he could. After that, I didn't want Webster to work in my store anymore. On the morning before the vandalism occurred, I notified Mike Webster by mail that he was fired. I was too scared to tell him to his face.

"You know what I think? I don't think there was any teenager who rushed in. I think it was Webster who wrecked the back room of my shop. I think he wanted to get back at me for firing him."

EXHIBIT A is the notice that was mailed to Webster. It was found in his pants pocket when he was arrested.

A lawyer for Mike Webster has given a different side of the story:

"Is James Bradley the nice guy he says he is? Or are there a lot of customers who might want to get even with him? It seems that Bradley has a history of improper store operation."

EXHIBIT B is a newspaper article which shows that James Bradley was ordered to close the previous pet shop he owned. During the time Bradley was operating his new store, he was sued three times by dissatisfied customers for selling them animals who turned out to be sickly. When the owners attempted to return the animals, Bradley refused to refund their money.

Mike Webster has given his side of the story:

"I think fish are the most beautiful animals in

the world, don't you? I have a big tank at home with dozens of little ones swimming around. Sure I was upset when I was fired. But it didn't stop me from caring for the goldfish in Mr. Bradley's store.

"I went back to the store that night because I had forgotten to feed the beautiful fish. When that crazy teenager rushed in, I just blacked out from fright."

Mike Webster's lawyer has entered into evidence EXHIBIT C, a photograph of the back room taken by the night watchman. You will note that as Webster fainted, he knocked over the fishbowl. The dead fish are lying near him.

The lawyer stated that if Webster had faked his fainting, he would never have knocked over the goldfish bowl as he pretended to fall. He was far too fond of fish.

Mike Webster's lawyer says his client is innocent. The damage was caused by an unknown teenage vandal who was an unhappy customer of the pet shop. His motive was to get back at Bradley for illegal business practices.

The lawyer for James Bradley claims that Mike Webster made up his story. He accuses Webster of pretending to faint when the night watchman was about to catch him wrecking the back room. There was no teenage vandal.

LADIES AND GENTLEMEN OF THE JURY:
You have just heard the Case of the Broken Goldfish Bowl. You must decide the merits of James Bradley's claim. Be sure to carefully examine the evidence in EXHIBITS A, B, and C.

Is Mike Webster guilty as charged? Or was the damage done by a teenage vandal?

Pets-R-People
PET SHOP

Concord Mall
Cherry Valley, New Jersey

August 16, 1988

Dear Mr. Webster:

This letter is to inform you that, effective today, we are no longer in need of
your services, and your employment has
ceased immediately.

Your final paycheck is enclosed.

Sincerely,

James Bradley

James Bradley

Pets-R-People

Pet store owner fined, barred from business

The owner of a pet shop in town was ordered yesterday to close permanently his store.

A Superior Court Judge also ordered James Bradley to pay $15,000 in fines and about $5,000 to dissatisfied customers. Bradley had been convicted of various animal neglect charges.

Last month Bradley admitted violating several state consumer protection laws. He also admitted he did not provide pedigree papers to customers and that he failed to post proper consumer protection warnings.

The penalties imposed are in addition to those levied earlier this week by a judge who fined him for 100 animal cruelty violations.

(Story continued on page 8.)

EXHIBIT C

VERDICT

MIKE WEBSTER CAUSED THE DAMAGE.

Webster claimed he fainted when the teenager entered the back room. But EXHIBIT C shows he was lying *on top* of some of the papers.

This would have been impossible unless the papers were on the floor *before* he fell—indicating it was Mike Webster who had vandalized the back room. He pretended to faint when the night watchman arrived.

YOU BE
THE JURY
Courtroom III

. . for Robby, again . . . .

Order in the Court

Ladies AND GENTLEMEN OF THE JURY:

This court is now in session. My name is Judge John Dennenberg. You are the jury, and the trials are set to begin.

You have a serious responsibility. Will the innocent be sent to jail and the guilty go free? Let's hope not. Your job is to make sure that justice is served.

Read each case carefully. Study the evidence presented and then decide.

GUILTY OR NOT GUILTY??

Both sides of the case will be presented to you. The person who has the complaint is called the *plaintiff*. He or she has brought the case to court. If a crime is involved, the State is the accuser.

The person being accused is called the *defendant*. The defendant is pleading his or her innocence and presents a much different version of what happened.

IN EACH CASE, THREE PIECES OF EVIDENCE WILL BE PRESENTED AS

179

EXHIBITS A, B, AND C. EXAMINE THE EXHIBITS VERY CAREFULLY. A *CLUE* TO THE SOLUTION OF EACH CASE WILL BE FOUND THERE. IT WILL DIRECTLY POINT TO THE INNOCENCE OR GUILT OF THE ACCUSED.

Remember, each side will try to convince you that his or her version is what actually happened. BUT YOU MUST MAKE THE FINAL DECISION.

The Case of
the Burning Barn

LADIES AND GENTLEMEN OF THE JURY:

When a fire occurs, and there is reason to believe it was purposely set to collect insurance, payment can be denied.

Today you are in court to decide on this issue.

Ezra Stiles, the plaintiff, is suing Oxford Insurance Company to collect insurance money for his barn, which was destroyed by fire. The company refuses to pay the claim. The insurance company's attorney thinks Mr. Stiles started the fire on purpose.

Ezra Stiles has given the following testimony:

"It was late in the evening of May 14. I've been a farmer all my life so I generally go to bed pretty early. All at once I heard this knocking on my door. I was half asleep by then and at first I thought I was just dreaming. When the knocking continued, I got up.

"I quickly threw on some clothes and ran downstairs. When I opened the door, there was Officer Conrad Darnoc. He told me he'd been driving by and seen flames coming from a window in my barn. He radioed for help and drove to the barn. There's a water spigot there, but he couldn't find a hose, so he drove up to the house to get help.

"Well, I grabbed the hose from my porch and we drove to my barn. By that time the fire had spread across one side of the barn. It was completely in flames."

EXHIBIT A is a photograph taken after the fire truck arrived.

Ezra Stiles is suing Oxford Insurance for $11,000, the cost of his barn. But the insurance company labels the blaze as suspicious.

The plaintiff thinks the insurance company is trying to avoid paying him. He believes the fire was set by a drifter who was seen in the area.

Mr. Stiles offers as proof EXHIBIT B, a report received by police several days earlier. It is a neighbor's complaint of a stranger who was seen wandering around the area the week of the fire.

Ezra Stiles continued his testimony:

"The day before the fire I found a few cigarette butts near my barn. There were also some empty food cans. I couldn't figure out how they got there."

The plaintiff claims the stranger may have used his barn as a place to sleep. He could have accidentally started the fire with a cigarette.

A lawyer for Oxford Insurance Company believes Stiles's actions at the time of the fire were very suspicious. They called Officer Darnoc to testify. First the question and then his answer:

Q: What did you do when you saw the fire?

A: I drove up the hill to Ezra Stiles's house. I thought I could use his hose until the fire truck arrived.

Q: How long did it take him to come to the door?

A: It was quite a while. I knocked and knocked, yelling for him to open the door. But there was no answer. I shouted and knocked for several minutes. Finally Stiles came to the door.

Q: What did he say when you told him about the fire?

A: Stiles was half dressed and he was rubbing his eyes. He said he had been sleeping.

The insurance company's lawyers claim a different reason Ezra Stiles took so long to answer the door. They believe he set the barn fire himself.

They claim that the farmer was down by his barn, spreading the fire, when he saw the policeman's car approaching. Under cover of darkness, he ran up a back road to his house, entered through the rear, and then opened the front door for Officer Darnoc.

The company's lawyers offer further proof in EXHIBIT C. It is a picture of the door of the barn. You will note that a wooden bar keeps the door closed.

If a stranger had accidentally started the fire inside the barn, he never would have bothered to lock the door before he fled.

The lawyers claim that Ezra Stiles had a good reason to start the fire. He recently had retired from farming. The barn was of little use to him.

Oxford Insurance Company believes the farmer set the fire as a means of collecting insurance money for a building that was no longer needed.

LADIES AND GENTLEMEN OF THE JURY:

You have just heard the Case of the Burning Barn. You must decide the merits of Ezra Stiles's claim. Be sure to carefully examine the evidence in EXHIBITS A, B, and C.

Was the barn fire started by a stranger? Or did the farmer start it to collect insurance money?

EXHIBIT A

EXHIBIT B

D.D.5

CRIME CLASSIFICATION	POLICE DEPARTMENT REPORT
SUSPICIOUS PERSON	

NAME OF COMPLAINANT	ADDRESS
BETTY MARGATE	712 CHESTNUT ROAD

May 10, 1989
7:46 am phone call. Complainant observed a stranger walking
down Chestnut Road, carrying a shopping bag filled with
clothing. A blanket was draped around his shoulders.

Stranger was male, 6ft tall and wearing dungarees and a blue
baseball cap.

Greg Banon

OFFICER ON DUTY

EXHIBIT C

VERDICT

THE FIRE WAS STARTED TO COLLECT INSURANCE MONEY.

In his testimony, the farmer said that when he was awakened, he quickly threw on some clothes and ran downstairs. EXHIBIT A shows Stiles at his barn half dressed. But his high boots are laced up.

If he had hurried to answer the door, he would not have had time to lace them.

While Ezra Stiles was setting the fire, he spotted Officer Darnoc. He quickly ran back to his house and threw *off* some clothes to make it look as though he had been sleeping.

But he forgot to unlace his boots.

The Case of
the Jelly Bean Jubilee

Ladies AND GENTLEMEN OF THE JURY:

When someone wins a contest by cheating, he or she is not entitled to keep the prize.

That is the point of law you must keep in mind today, as you decide to whom a contest prize rightfully belongs.

Curt Barr, the plaintiff, is suing Wendy Darling, the defendant, for the prize of a TV set. He claims she won it by cheating. But Wendy Darling says she won the prize fair and square.

Mr. Noel Roxy has testified as follows on behalf of the plaintiff:

"I'm Noel Roxy. That's right, the one and only Noel Roxy, owner of the fabulous Roxy Movie Palace. You've heard our slogan — 'Come to the Roxy, where everyone's a star!'

"During the week of October 18, we held a contest to advertise our fabulous new movie, *Jack and the Jelly Beanstalk.* We decided to call our contest the Jelly Bean Jubilee."

In the lobby of the theater was a large jar holding hundreds of jelly beans. The theater offered a TV to the person who most closely guessed the number of jelly beans in the jar.

The contest drew a large crowd. On the final day of the movie, the contest winner was announced.

When Noel Roxy opened the ballots, he was surprised to find that there were two winners. The jar held exactly 1,700 jelly beans. Wendy Darling guessed there were 1,750 in the jar. Curt Barr's guess was 1,650.

Since both persons were equally close, Mr. Roxy announced a playoff.

He had another bean jar in his office. He would bring it on the stage the next day. Each would guess the number of jelly beans inside the new jar. The winner of the tiebreaker would get the TV.

The day of the tiebreaker, both winners were called on stage. To everyone's amazement, Wendy Darling guessed the exact number of jelly beans in the jar — 2,240. Curt Barr's guess was far off.

Barr was disappointed. After the movie, he met the theater owner in the lobby. Mr. Roxy invited the young man to his second floor office for a recount.

When they entered the office, Curt Barr noticed that the window was open and an outside ladder was leaning against the sill.

Mr. Roxy was shocked. Someone had used the ladder to get into his office.

Curt Barr, the plaintiff, claims it could only have been Wendy Darling. He says she must have sneaked into the office the morning of the tie-breaker and counted the jelly beans ahead of time.

EXHIBIT A is a photograph of the office as it appeared when Barr and Roxy entered it.

I will read from the testimony of Noel Roxy. First the question and then his answer:

Q: Could anyone walk into your office while the second jelly bean jar was there?

A: That was impossible. I'm the only one with a key. The contest drew a lot of publicity, so I carefully locked the door each time I left the office.

Q: Had you kept your window locked, too?

A: I'm not sure. The window was definitely closed. But I'm not sure if it was locked.

Q: When you went into your office to bring the jelly bean jar to the stage, was the ladder leaning against the open window?

A: I didn't notice. But it must have been there.

Q: Did you lock your office door when you brought the jar to the stage?

A: No. There was no need to. I had the jar.

Q: Can you identify the ladder?

A: Yes. It's the one we keep in a checkroom in our lobby.

As further proof that Wendy Darling cheated, the plaintiff has entered this additional photo-

191

graph of the office as EXHIBIT B. He calls your attention to the stool near the bookcase. The bookshelf where Noel Roxy kept the second jelly bean jar is marked with an "X."

Ms. Darling was too short to reach the jar. Curt Barr contends that she moved the stool over to the bookshelf to reach the jar.

But afterwards, she forgot to remove the accusing evidence — the stool.

Wendy Darling insists that she didn't cheat. She says she won the TV set honestly and refuses to give it back.

She says the ladder was put in the window by Barr to make it look like she broke into the office. Everyone knew that he was upset when he lost the contest.

Ms. Darling suggested another version of what happened:

"I think Curt Barr planted the ladder and stool to make it look like I cheated. He thought he could get away with it. He thought no one would believe I guessed the exact number of jelly beans."

She claims that after Barr lost the tiebreaker, he took the ladder from the theater's checkroom and carried it up to the owner's office. Then he dropped it from the window to the ground. It looked like someone had climbed up the ladder and into the office.

As proof of her claim, Ms. Darling showed EXHIBIT C, a photograph of the back stairs door leading from the checkroom to the owner's office. Barr could have carried the ladder upstairs without being seen.

LADIES AND GENTLEMEN OF THE JURY:
You have just heard the Case of the Jelly Bean Jubilee. You must decide the merits of Curt Barr's claim. Be sure to carefully examine the evidence in EXHIBITS A, B, and C.

Did Wendy Darling secretly climb into the office and count the jelly beans? Or was the ladder placed there by Barr after he lost the contest?

EXHIBIT A

EXHIBIT C

VERDICT

THE LADDER WAS PLACED IN THE WINDOW AFTER THE CONTEST.

EXHIBIT A shows the ladder in Mr. Roxy's window. Notice that the window swings *outwards*. It would have been impossible for Wendy Darling to lean an outside ladder against the windowsill and climb up it. The top of the ladder would have prevented the window from opening.

After the tiebreaker, Curt Barr carried a ladder up to the office, opened the window, and slipped it outside, leaning one end against the sill.

The Case of
the Sports Superstar

LADIES AND GENTLEMEN OF THE JURY:

When a person's picture is used in an advertisement without permission, even if that person is a famous public figure, it is an invasion of that person's privacy.

Such is the case before you today.

Byron "Lefty" Ward, the plaintiff, was once the leading pitcher in the National Baseball League. He is suing TV station KBB for illegally using his name and picture to advertise a TV sports event. KBB, the defendant, claims they used Ward's picture with the star's permission.

Wink Hastings of TV station KBB has testified as follows:

"Wink Hastings is my name and TV is my game. I'm the station manager at KBB.

"When KBB got the rights to televise Weston College baseball games, we wanted to attract as many viewers as possible. Then one morning, I got this brilliant idea. They don't call me 'Quick-as-a-

Wink' Hastings for nothing. I realized that if we could hire Byron Ward as our announcer, more people would watch the games."

Hastings met with Ward. The baseball star said he was very interested. Byron Ward signed a letter of agreement stating he would accept the job if the TV station could work out an agreeable contract.

This letter was entered as EXHIBIT A.

During their next meeting, the two men argued over the terms of the agreement. Wink Hastings was under pressure. The day of the first game was approaching. KBB had to begin its advertising campaign.

Byron Ward finally walked out of the talks, stating he had changed his mind. He didn't want to work for KBB. But by that time the advertisement with Ward's picture was in newspapers. It said he was announcing the games.

Byron Ward claims the advertisement damaged his reputation. His fans expected to see him as announcer and they were disappointed.

Byron Ward testified about his dealings with Wink Hastings and KBB. First the question and then his answer:

Q: Is this your signature on the letter?
A: Yes, it is. But Mr. Hastings knew I would announce the games only if he met my terms.

The wording in the letter says so.

Q: Why didn't you take the job?

A: I didn't like Hastings's attitude. First he told me he would pay me a lot of money. Later he changed his mind. I got so disgusted that I told him I didn't want to work for his TV station.

Q: Did you pose for the picture in the ad and give KBB permission to use it?

A: No, I certainly did not.

EXHIBIT B is the advertisement that is the reason for Byron Ward's legal action against KBB. It is a photograph of Byron Ward seated behind a KBB microphone.

Wink Hastings told the court a completely different story:

"When I first suggested the announcing job to Ward, he was very interested.

"I told him we needed to prepare an advertising campaign immediately and he agreed to pose for it. We had his permission.

"But when it got down to details, Ward became unreasonable. Besides wanting a higher salary, he insisted we buy him a new wardrobe. He wanted a different suit for every game. He also said he needed a private dressing room.

"We just couldn't afford his demands. By the time we decided we couldn't work things out, it was too late to stop the advertisement."

Byron Ward states that the station manager is lying. He claims that the picture in the advertisement is a complete fake. He never posed for it.

Ward claims that since KBB needed to prepare the ad before they had a final agreement, someone else posed behind a KBB microphone. Then the artist glued on a photograph of the celebrity's head.

To prove his accusation, Ward explained to the court how he thinks the photograph was made:

"They cut out my head from a photograph taken when I was still playing baseball. Then they glued it onto a photograph of someone else."

Mr. Ward showed the court EXHIBIT C. He believes this is the photograph the artist used to create the picture of him sitting at the mike.

Byron Ward continued his testimony:

"Notice the similarities between my face on the picture in uniform and my face in the ad. KBB eliminated the lock of hair hanging down my forehead. They knew announcers had to have a neater look.

"I never posed for the advertisement. It's an obvious phony, made up from my photograph."

LADIES AND GENTLEMEN OF THE JURY: You have just heard the Case of the Sports

Superstar. You must decide the merits of Mr. Ward's claim. Be sure to carefully examine the evidence in EXHIBITS A, B, and C.

Was the advertisement for KBB prepared with Byron Ward's permission? Or did the TV station use a fake ad?

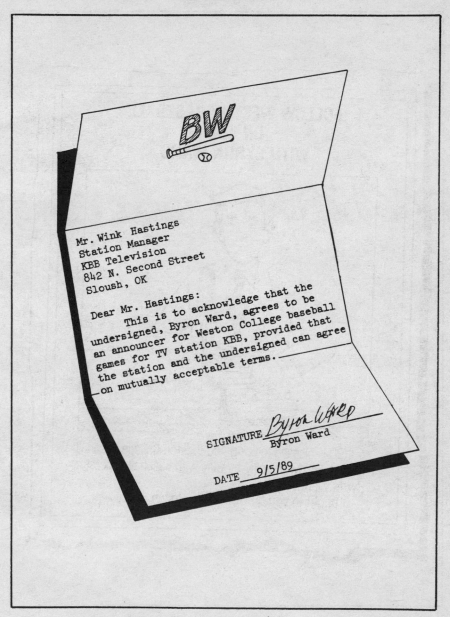

Mr. Wink Hastings
Station Manager
KBB Television
842 N. Second Street
Sloush, OK

Dear Mr. Hastings:

This is to acknowledge that the undersigned, Byron Ward, agrees to be an announcer for Weston College baseball games for TV station KBB, provided that the station and the undersigned can agree on mutually acceptable terms.

SIGNATURE *Byron Ward*
Byron Ward

DATE 9/5/89

**FOLLOW WESTON BASEBALL
ON KBB
WITH BYRON WARD**

KBB is pleased to bring you Weston College baseball games. Follow the play-by-play with baseball superstar Byron Ward.

Brought to you by BUZZ OFF Roach Spray.

EXHIBIT C

VERDICT

THE ADVERTISEMENT WAS A FAKE.

EXHIBIT C shows Byron Ward wearing a *left-handed* baseball glove (on his right hand). And Ward's signature on the letter in EXHIBIT A has a slant often seen in the penmanship of left-handed writers. So Byron Ward *was a lefty*.

But the advertisement in EXHIBIT B shows a photo of Ward writing with his *right* hand.

Byron "Lefty" Ward never posed for the ad.

The Case of
the Disappearing Shopper

LADIES AND GENTLEMEN OF THE JURY:

Shoplifting is the act of taking merchandise from a store without paying for it. The store must have proof the person intended to steal the property.

Keep this issue of proof in mind as you examine the case before you today.

Flash Appliances, the plaintiff, accuses Donald Hill, the defendant, of shoplifting a stereo-radio from its store. Hill claims he is innocent and carried the radio out of the store to help a stranger. He says the stranger had tricked him.

Benjamin Gunn, a store guard, has testified as follows:

"My name is Ben Gunn, and I'm a security guard at Flash Appliances. Saturday, July 8, was a busy shopping day for us. It was raining, and the bad weather kept people indoors.

"At approximately 3:10 P.M., there was a bright flash of lightning followed by a loud thunderclap. All the store's lights went out.

"You can't be too careful when the power goes

207

out. That's why I moved to the front of the store and stood by the exit door.

"When the lights came back on, I saw this boxed radio by the door. I figured that while the lights were out, someone took the radio from a shelf, carried it past the cashier's counter, and put it in a convenient place where it could be taken out without paying.

"Then the rain stopped. No one touched the radio at first. But then, about ten minutes later, I saw this man, Donald Hill, pick up the box and carry it out to the parking lot. I stopped him just before he got to his car and held him there until the police arrived."

EXHIBIT A is a photograph of the two men, taken after the police arrived. They are standing next to Hill's car.

Mr. Hill insists he was not in the store when the lights went out. He testified as follows:

"I live about a mile from Flash. When the rain stopped, I wanted to go jogging. But my Walkman needed new batteries. So I drove over to the store to get some.

"I pulled into a parking space. A woman had just left the store and was carrying packages to her car. It was next to mine.

"She had trouble holding the packages and finding the car keys in her purse. I asked if she needed help.

"The lady told me she could manage, but she

had left a package by the exit door. She said I could save her a trip if I would bring it out.

"That's when I went into the store and walked over to the exit door. I picked up the box and carried it outside.

"When I looked for her car, the woman was gone. All of a sudden the guard stopped me."

Lawyers for the store challenged Donald Hill's story. First their question and then Hill's answer:

Q: Didn't it seem strange that there was no store sticker on the box you took, to show the merchandise was paid for?

A: I never really noticed. I was only trying to do a good deed.

Q: Did the other packages the woman carried to her car have paid stickers on them?

A: I remember seeing them. They're so big it's hard to miss.

Q: How can you account for the woman's disappearance?

A: I guess she saw the store guard following me and knew she would be caught. So she just drove away.

The store's lawyers entered as EXHIBIT B a sample of a "paid" sticker on an appliance box. The store uses these stickers as security so they know when merchandise has been paid for.

The store's lawyers went on to say that the

police have been unable to locate the person whom Hill says he was helping. The lawyers claim there never was such a person.

Donald Hill's lawyer stated that the woman was the one who committed the crime. She tricked Hill into carrying out the radio.

Hill's lawyer further claimed that the store lacks sufficient proof. Since the radio was moved while the lights were out, Flash Appliances must prove Mr. Hill was in the store at the time.

Hill's attorney showed EXHIBIT C, a diagram of the front of the store. The entrance door is very close to the exit door. EXHIBIT C shows that it was possible for Donald Hill to walk through the entrance door after the lights went back on and go directly to the exit door. He could have done this without being seen by the guard.

LADIES AND GENTLEMEN OF THE JURY:
You have just heard the Case of the Disappearing Shopper. You must decide the merits of Flash Appliances's claim. Be sure to carefully examine the evidence in EXHIBITS A, B, and C.

Was Donald Hill tricked into taking the stereo-radio? Or did he steal it?

EXHIBIT A

EXHIBIT C

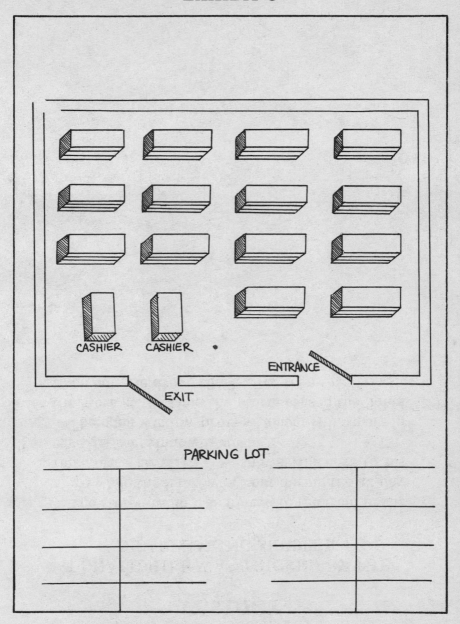

VERDICT

DONALD HILL WAS TRICKED BY THE DISAPPEARING SHOPPER.

The stereo-radio was moved to the front of the store while the lights were out during the all-day rainstorm. EXHIBIT A shows Hill next to his car. His car window is *open*.

The open window proves Donald Hill wasn't in the store at the time the storm caused the lights to go out. He drove there after the rain stopped.

The Case of
the Squished Tomatoes

LADIES AND GENTLEMEN OF THE JURY:

If a burglary takes place, and a great deal of money is stolen, the thief may be sent to prison for a very long time.

Carefully consider this serious penalty as you listen to the evidence presented here today.

Since we are in criminal court today, the State is the accuser. The State accuses Andrew Turner, the defendant, of stealing $2,000 from the safe of the Hopp-n-Shop Grocery Store. Andrew Turner, who works at Hopp-n-Shop, insists he is innocent.

The State called Harvey Hopp as its first witness.

"My name is Harvey Hopp. I own the Hopp-n-Shop Grocery Store. On the evening of June 5, at approximately 9:15 P.M., I locked up the store for the night and headed home. I learned later that at 9:56 P.M., the burglar alarm for the store's safe went off. Luckily the police responded immediately."

EXHIBIT A is an official record of the burglar alarm report.

When the police arrived, they discovered that

the back door of the store was unlocked. In searching the store, they found the office safe open. The money inside had been stolen.

In a corner of the store, near a vegetable bin, police found a basket of spilled tomatoes.

The thief had left his mark. Damaged tomatoes, some half eaten, were on the floor. On a large wall mirror, scrawled in the juice of a squished tomato, the thief had written the word "DELICIOUS!"

EXHIBIT B is a photograph of the damage done by the thief.

The State questioned Harvey Hopp further. First the question and then his answer:

Q: Are you positive you locked the front and back door of the store on the evening of the burglary?

A: I'm certain I did. I've followed the same routine for years.

Q: Did anyone have the combination to your safe?

A: I'm the only one. But it's possible that someone who worked for me could have seen me open the safe and remembered the combination.

Q: Does anyone else use your office?

A: No. I'm the only one. But sometimes my workers come in if they want to speak with me privately.

Since there was no evidence that the back door

was broken into, police reasoned the burglary was an inside job.

They believed that one of Hopp's workers could have hidden in the store before closing. Then, when the owner locked the store for the night, the thief came out of hiding. He had the store all to himself.

Inside the office wastebasket, near the safe, police discovered a half-eaten sandwich.

The sandwich was sent to the crime lab for examination. A slice of cheese from the sandwich revealed important evidence. There were unusual teeth marks made by the person biting into it.

The police lab report is shown in EXHIBIT C.

The bite marks revealed that the person eating the sandwich had a center tooth missing. It showed the width of his front teeth and the spaces between them.

The teeth marks from the cheese were compared with those of the people who worked in the store. Andrew Turner's teeth marks matched exactly.

His middle tooth is missing and all other teeth matched the marks in the cheese.

On this basis, Andrew Turner was placed under arrest and is on trial here today.

Turner had worked for Mr. Hopp for seven months. But recently there was friction between them. It seemed Turner loved to eat. He constantly nibbled on store food without paying for it.

The State questioned Andrew Turner about his eating habits:

"Food? Sure I love food. Anyone can see that. Just look at the size of my stomach. I love to nibble.

"But I hate tomatoes. I'm allergic to them. Every time I eat a tomato my eyes get watery and I break out in a rash."

The defendant was asked to account for the half-eaten sandwich found in the wastebasket. The following is from his testimony:

"I admit it. That's the sandwich I ate. But I didn't eat it the night of the burglary. I got hungry in the late afternoon. I know Mr. Hopp doesn't like me eating. So I sneaked in his office while he was in the front of the store and gobbled up a fantastic sandwich. When I saw Hopp coming, I tossed the last of it in his wastebasket."

Andrew Turner's lawyer claims that at the time the safe alarm rang, Andrew was at home talking on the telephone to his girlfriend, Nancy King.

Nancy King supported the defendant's story. Miss King said they talked on the phone for about a half hour, although she was not sure of the exact time of the call.

Andrew Turner's lawyer claims that the testimony of Andrew's girlfriend provides the defendant with an alibi. And since Turner is allergic to tomatoes, it is further proof of his innocence.

LADIES AND GENTLEMEN OF THE JURY: You have just heard the Case of the Squished Tomatoes. You must decide the merits of the State's accusation. Be sure to carefully examine the evidence in EXHIBITS A, B, and C.

Did Andrew Turner steal the money from the Hopp-n-Shop's safe? Or was he innocent?

EXHIBIT A

D.D. 8

POLICE DEPARTMENT BURGLAR ALARM REPORT	PRECINCT 18th
	REPORT NUMBER 842A

DATE June 5, 1989

TIME 9:56 pm

LOCATION Hopp-n-Shopp Grocery Store
82 Prospect St.

Police car #6 dispatched.

Monique Vespucci

OFFICER ON DUTY

EXHIBIT C

POLICE
DEPARTMENT
LABORATORY
REPORT

REFERENCE
Hopp-n-Shopp
Grocery Store
82 Prospect St.

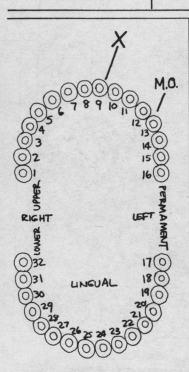

X

M.O.

RIGHT   LEFT

LOWER   UPPER   PERMAMENT

LINGUAL

REPORT ON PARTIAL SANDWICH
FOUND IN WASTEBASKET

CONTENTS OF SANDWICH

Sandwich contained cheese, ham,
onions, hot green peppers, cucumbers
on white bread. Thick layer of
catsup on upper slice of bread.

DESCRIPTION OF BITE MARKS

Teeth marks in cheese reveal
the following:
Upper left central incisor missing
(#9). Malocclusion of upper left
first bicuspid (#13). Other teeth
of normal size.

Harry Whitcomb, Ph.D.
LABORATORY DIRECTOR

VERDICT

ANDREW TURNER BROKE INTO THE SAFE.

Turner testified that he couldn't be the burglar because he was allergic to tomatoes. In EXHIBIT C, the lab report describes the sandwich Turner was eating. It was topped with *catsup*.

Turner admitted it was his sandwich, but forgot that catsup is made from tomatoes. Andrew Turner really wasn't allergic to tomatoes.

It was Turner who opened the safe and scrawled the sign on the mirror.

The Case of the Missing Talk-Show Host

LADIES AND GENTLEMEN OF THE JURY:

Kidnapping is a serious crime in which someone carries away and holds a person against his or her will.

Since we are in criminal court today, the State is the accuser. The State charges Rudy Reddy, the owner of Reddy Roofing Company, with kidnapping Edward "Action" Jackson. Mr. Reddy, the defendant, says he was never involved in the kidnapping. Furthermore, he thinks the kidnapping was a fake.

Edward Jackson has testified as follows:

"Hello, everybody! This is Edward 'Action' Jackson, your WZEB Action Man, here to answer all your phone calls about... Oh, I'm sorry, sometimes I get a little carried away. Let me start again.

"My name is Edward Jackson. I'm the Action Man on radio station WZEB. My program is a telephone call-in show that gives advice to callers about practically anything.

"On my radio program of October 24, I received a phone call from Mrs. Betty Harcourt. Mrs. Harcourt complained that she had paid Reddy Roofing Company to have her roof repaired. But the roof still leaked and the company refused to fix it.

"I suggested that she place the following sign on her front lawn:

MY ROOF WAS POORLY REPAIRED BY

REDDY ROOFING COMPANY

AND IT STILL LEAKS!

Jackson's advice worked. The first day the sign was up, Rudy Reddy immediately went to Mrs. Harcourt's house to repair the roof. But because of the publicity, Reddy's business fell off badly. He was angry at Edward Jackson.

One morning, about a week after the radio program, a note appeared in the mailbox of station WZEB.

The note is entered as EXHIBIT A. It states that Edward Jackson had been kidnapped and would be returned only if $50,000 were paid in ransom.

When the radio station owner, Rhonda Braver, received the ransom note, she decided not to contact the police. Instead, she withdrew money from the bank and dropped it off at the location specified in the note.

The following afternoon, Edward Jackson walked into the radio station. It was three days after the alleged kidnapping. His suit was wrinkled and dirty. There was a bump on his head.

Jackson said he had escaped. He had been held in the woods inside a shed that was a mile from the radio station.

Police went to the location where the ransom money was placed. The money was still there. The kidnapper never picked it up.

Mr. Jackson described to the court how he was kidnapped:

"After my radio show Monday evening, I went to the parking lot to get my car. It was pretty dark out.

"As I opened the car door, someone grabbed me from behind. He covered my mouth and hit me on the head. I must have fainted.

"When I woke up, I found myself tied to a chair with a bandana over my eyes. I managed to loosen it by rubbing it against my shoulder. I found myself in a dark shed. No one was around.

"My head was throbbing with pain. I must have been unconscious for a long time. I felt tired and dirty. I hadn't washed or brushed my teeth for days. I was starved.

"It took some time, but I was able to untie the knots that bound me to the chair. Then I escaped."

EXHIBIT B is a photograph of Edward Jackson taken when police arrived at the radio station.

The police crime lab analyzed the black smudges on Jackson's face and clothing. They found it was a tar used for roof repair. On the strength of this evidence, Rudy Reddy was arrested.

The lawyer for the defendant admits that Reddy was very upset with Jackson. But he states that his client had nothing to do with the kidnapping.

He believes the kidnapping was actually a fake.

He points to the police report, EXHIBIT C. When Jackson returned to the radio station, he still had his wristwatch and wallet. Rudy Reddy's lawyer says that if Edward Jackson really had been kidnapped, his valuables would have been taken.

Mr. Reddy's lawyer continued:

"The popularity of Edward Jackson's radio show had been slipping badly. It was once the most-listened-to show on radio. But in recent months a quiz show on another station was attracting his audience.

"Jackson's kidnapping made the front page of the local newspaper. Everyone talked about it.

"It was great publicity for him. His popularity began to rise again after the kidnapping. More people than ever began listening to his show."

The lawyer for the defense states that Edward Jackson purposely faked the kidnapping for the publicity.

LADIES AND GENTLEMEN OF THE JURY:
You have just heard the Case of the Missing

Talk-Show Host. You are to decide the merit of the State's accusation. Be sure to carefully examine the evidence in EXHIBITS A, B, and C.

Did Rudy Reddy kidnap Edward Jackson? Or was the incident a publicity stunt?

EXHIBIT C

D.D. 12

CRIME CLASSIFICATION KIDNAPPING	POLICE DEPARTMENT SUPPLEMENTARY REPORT	PRECINCT 12th
DATE November 4, 1988		REPORT NUMBER 296-C

    The officers below arrived at radio station WZEB at 1:37 pm. The station owner, Rhonda Braver, reported that one of her employees, Edward "Action" Jackson had been kidnapped on November 1 and had found his way back to the radio station.

    Jackson's forehead had a bruise upper right and he was disheveled. His wallet and wristwatch were in his possession. No valuables were taken.

    Braver claims a $50,000 ransom was paid. Braver and Jackson were taken to police headquarters for further questioning.

Fred Hangrove
OFFICER

M. Bogent
OFFICER

231

VERDICT

THE KIDNAPPING WAS A FAKE.

Jackson had been missing for three days. He testified he was tired and dirty. EXHIBIT B is a photograph of Jackson when he walked into the radio station, after his escape.

Despite the smudges on his face, Jackson didn't have a three-day beard. *He must have shaved.*

Edward Jackson faked the kidnapping and hid at home. He made himself up to look as though he had escaped from the shed. But he forgot about the beard.

The Case of
the Nosy Neighbor

LADIES AND GENTLEMEN OF THE JURY:

All of us have the right to personal privacy. When we are in our homes we should be protected from nosy neighbors.

The residents of Freemont Terrace are in court today and have charged Penny Parker with snooping and interfering with their right to privacy. Ms. Parker, the defendant, says she is only interested in her neighbors' welfare and never bothers them.

Gordon Winslow of Freemont Terrace has testified as follows:

"Uhhh ... my name is Gordon ... Gordon Winslow. I'm a little nervous ... I've never been in a courtroom before. I live on Freemont Terrace.

"Freemont Terrace is a quiet little street lined with small houses. Most of us residents have lived there for years. We're quiet people.

"Eight months ago, Penny Parker moved into the neighborhood. She recently had retired from her job.

"She didn't make any friends. But everyone on

Freemont Terrace knew she was there. She often sat by her living room window watching her neighbors come and go. No matter where we went, Penny Parker was watching us."

Soon after Penny Parker moved in, people found mysterious letters in their mailboxes.

One homeowner received a note saying he should cut his grass more often. Another was told to keep the lid on her garbage can because it smelled.

One weekend, Gordon Winslow was sitting by his fireplace watching a soccer game on TV. During a commercial break, he went to the kitchen to fix a snack.

As he opened the refrigerator door, Winslow heard a noise outside his kitchen window. He turned around and saw a person's outline behind his window shade. Beneath it, a pair of binoculars was peering in at him.

EXHIBIT A is a view of the window from Winslow's kitchen.

Gordon Winslow ran outside, but by that time the intruder was gone.

He searched the area. In the flower bed below the window he found a handkerchief. On it were the initials "PP."

Mr. Winslow immediately took a photograph to show where the hanky was found. This photograph is entered in evidence as EXHIBIT B.

Gordon Winslow was very annoyed. He met with

neighbors and they voted to take legal action against Penny Parker. They have asked the court to order the defendant to stop bothering them.

Mr. Winslow testified as follows. First the question and then his answer:

Q: Did you recognize the person at the window?

A: No, I didn't. The shade was down, except for a space at the bottom. All I could see was an outline and a pair of binoculars.

Q: Why do you believe it was Ms. Parker?

A: It was definitely an outline of a woman's head. It must have been her. She's a terrible busybody. She knows when you're going to sneeze even before you do.

Q: What time did you go into your kitchen?

A: It was around 2:30 in the afternoon.

Q: How do you know the hanky hadn't been lying there for days?

A: I was puttering in my yard that morning and cleaned out the flower bed. It wasn't there then.

Penny Parker says that her neighbor is mistaken. She never peeked through Gordon Winslow's window. She testified as follows:

"I wish the people of Freemont Terrace would understand I'm only looking out for their own good.

"Many of them work. They should be glad to

have a nice person like me watching out for the neighborhood."

Penny Parker says the hanky was hers and she could explain how it got there:

"I was taking my daily walk along a path that cuts through the rear of Freemont Terrace. It was around noon. It was cold out and a strong wind was blowing. I was wearing my coat and hat.

"All of a sudden a gust of wind blew my hat off and into Mr. Winslow's yard. So I ran after it.

"My hat landed in his flower bed. I picked it up and went on my way. The hanky must have fallen out of my pocket."

EXHIBIT C is the hanky found by Mr. Winslow and which the defendant identifies as hers.

Penny Parker continued her testimony:

"I never looked into his window. It must have been someone else. I was home at 2:30 when Winslow said it happened. I may be interested in my neighbors' welfare. But I'm not *that* kind of person."

Penny Parker asks that the action against her be dismissed. She likes her neighbors and says they are mistaken to think she is nosy.

LADIES AND GENTLEMEN OF THE JURY:
You have just heard the Case of the Nosy Neighbor. You must decide the merits of the claim

against Penny Parker. Be sure to carefully examine the evidence in EXHIBITS A, B, and C.

Was Penny Parker the nosy neighbor who peeked into Gordon Winslow's kitchen window? Or was it someone else?

EXHIBIT B

EXHIBIT C

VERDICT

PENNY PARKER WAS THE NOSY NEIGHBOR.

In her testimony, Ms. Parker said she had dropped the hanky when her hat blew into Winslow's flower bed earlier that day.

But the chimney smoke in EXHIBIT B shows that the wind was blowing *away* from Winslow's house. Therefore, Parker's hat could not have been blown into the flower bed. It would have blown in the opposite direction.

Penny Parker made up the story to explain how the hanky got there.

The Case of
the Hotel Break-in

LADIES AND GENTLEMEN OF THE JURY:

If a hotel provides a safety deposit box for guests, it is not responsible for property that is stolen from their rooms. But if a hotel worker steals the property, that may be a different matter.

That is the point of law you must keep in mind today as you decide whether an employee was responsible for a hotel theft.

Donna Smith, the plaintiff, is a traveling salesperson for the Vega Jewelry Company. She is suing the Erbamont Hotel. She claims that while she was in the lobby, one of the hotel's workers stole a jewelry case from her hotel room.

The lawyer for the hotel claims the theft was not done by a hotel worker. He believes that when Donna Smith discovered her jewelry case had been stolen, she made it look like a hotel worker was responsible, so she could sue the hotel.

Donna Smith has testified as follows:

"My name is Donna Smith. I'm a sales representative for Vega Jewelry. On the afternoon of Thursday, October 21, I checked into the Erbamont Hotel. When I got to my room, I saw a notice on the wall that said:

THIS HOTEL DOES NOT ACCEPT LIABILITY FOR LOSS OR DAMAGE TO GUESTS' PROPERTY. VALUABLES MAY BE STORED IN SAFETY DEPOSIT BOXES AT THE FRONT DESK.

"I carry a lot of valuable jewelry samples with me so I went right back down to the front desk to find out about a safety deposit box. I left my jewelry case in my room."

When Smith returned to her room she took a nap. Upon waking, she discovered her case was gone. It contained more than $25,000 in jewelry samples.

I will now quote from the testimony of Ms. Smith. First the question and then her answer:

Q: What floor was your hotel room on?

A: On the sixth floor, next to the housekeeping closet. I think that's where the hotel's sheets and towels are stored.

Q: Can you describe the layout of your hotel room?

A: The door to my room opens onto the hallway. But the room has an extra door. That door goes into the housekeeping closet.

EXHIBIT A is a diagram of the sixth floor. Note the hallway door to Smith's room and the side door between her room and the housekeeping closet.

Donna Smith continued her testimony:

Q: Can your room be entered from that house-keeping closet?

A: No. There is a bolt on the door. It can only be unlocked from inside my room.

Q: What happened after you returned from the front desk?

A: I went to my room and took a quick nap. When I woke up I looked around for my jewelry case. I couldn't believe it was missing.

When the police arrived they discovered that someone had punched a hole in the side door of Donna Smith's hotel room right near the bolt. A wire had been inserted into the hole.

Donna Smith's lawyer described how the theft occurred. He explained that only hotel workers had a key to the closet. He believes that one of them entered the housekeeping closet, punched out the hole, inserted a wire, and slipped it around the bolt in Smith's room. The intruder then pulled the bolt open and entered the room.

EXHIBIT B is a photograph of the hole and wire as seen from Smith's room.

Donna Smith's lawyer also has entered as evidence EXHIBIT C. It is a photograph of the door as seen from inside the housekeeping closet. The blurred fingerprints on the door show where the thief punched out the hole.

The hotel's lawyer acknowledges that the jewelry was stolen. But she claims it was not an employee who stole it.

The lawyer believes that while Smith was at the front desk, an unknown thief was able to break into her room through the main hallway door. The thief took the jewelry and fled.

In his testimony, Dudley Nelson, the hotel manager, explained his version of the robbery. First the question and then his answer:

Q: What makes you think Donna Smith altered the evidence to make it look like a hotel worker committed the theft?

A: It has to do with the time after Ms. Smith left the front desk. She didn't report the robbery for nearly half an hour. She said she took a nap before she discovered the theft, but I don't believe her.

Q: Why do you think she waited so long?

A: When she saw the jewelry was missing, she thought up a plan to blame someone from the hotel. Smith slipped out of the hotel and bought tools from a nearby hardware store. Then she returned to her room and made the hole.

Erbamont Hotel stands by its explanation. It

believes the theft was committed by an outsider and the hotel is not responsible for the stolen jewelry.

LADIES AND GENTLEMEN OF THE JURY:
You have just heard the Case of the Hotel Break-in. You must decide the merits of Donna Smith's evidence in EXHIBITS A, B, and C.

Did a hotel worker break into the plaintiff's room? Or did Donna Smith make it look that way?

EXHIBIT A

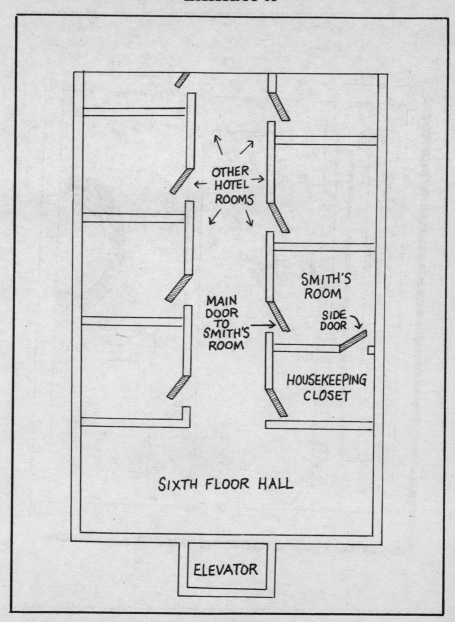

OTHER HOTEL ROOMS

SMITH'S ROOM

MAIN DOOR TO SMITH'S ROOM

SIDE DOOR

HOUSEKEEPING CLOSET

SIXTH FLOOR HALL

ELEVATOR

EXHIBIT B

EXHIBIT C

VERDICT

A HOTEL WORKER BROKE INTO
THE ROOM.

The hole in the door was made from inside the housekeeping closet. The edges of a hole made in wood on the side where a sharp tool enters the wood will be smooth. But the edges will be rough on the opposite side where the tool punctures through.

In EXHIBIT B, the rough and splintered edges around the hole are inside Donna Smith's room. On the opposite side of the door in EXHIBIT C, the edges are smooth.

If Smith had made the hole, the splinters would have appeared on the opposite side of the door.

The Case of
the Barking Dog

LADIES AND GENTLEMEN OF THE JURY:

The owner of a pet must make sure that his or her animal behaves. If a pet damages someone's property, the owner is expected to pay. However, there must be proof that the animal actually caused the damage.

Please keep this issue of proof in mind as you decide the case before you today.

Ann Potter, the plaintiff, has charged that Norma Winkler's terrier injured her pet goose and caused other damage. Norma Winkler, the defendant, says that Mrs. Potter is mistaken. The injury was caused by a wild raccoon.

For her birthday present, Mrs. Winkler's husband surprised her with a pet terrier. She named the dog "Lady."

Ann Potter has testified as follows:

"My name is Ann Potter and I just love animals, don't you? But my most favorite animals are geese. I just go 'ga-ga' for geese. I have four geese that

I've raised in my backyard, and I sell baby geese, which are called goslings, for pets.

"On the afternoon of July 8, I was in my bedroom and heard some noises in the backyard. My geese were honking and I heard the loud barking of a dog.

"I hurried downstairs. The yard was empty. Then I ran over to the cage where I keep my four geese.

"There was Hugo lying on the ground. He was badly hurt. Hugo's leg was broken and his tail feathers were missing. The feathers were scattered all over the yard.

"Then I knew why I had heard a dog barking. It was Norma Winkler's pet terrier, Lady, who was responsible."

On a wooden table in a corner of the cage, Mrs. Potter kept her geese's eggs. The eggs were on the ground, all of them broken.

EXHIBIT A is a photograph of the broken eggs.

Mrs. Potter is suing for the money she paid the veterinarian to fix Hugo's leg. She claims she also is owed $50 for the broken eggs that were knocked over by Lady. When the eggs hatched she could have sold the goslings for $5.00 each.

Ann Potter was questioned by Norma Winkler's lawyer. First the question and then her answer:

Q: Did you actually see Lady in your yard?

A: No. But I'd recognize her bark anywhere. It was definitely Lady's barking. My geese get excited when they're scared. They start to honk.

Q: Did you see any other animals in your yard? For instance, did you see a raccoon?

A: No. I can't see the cage from my bedroom window.

Q: When you ran into your yard, did you see Lady?

A: The yard was empty. I must have scared Lady off. She probably slipped through the hole in my fence.

EXHIBIT B is a photograph of the hole in Mrs. Potter's backyard fence where the dog could have entered.

Norma Winkler insists that it wasn't Lady who did the damage. But she admits that Lady was in her neighbor's yard earlier on the day that the damage occurred.

Mrs. Winkler testified as follows:

"I let Lady outside every morning and watch her from my doorway. She's well trained, you know.

"That morning I saw Lady run over to Ann Potter's house. I chased after her, but she slipped through the hole in the Potters' fence. I called Lady and she came back out and jumped into my arms. She was only in the yard for a minute."

Mrs. Winkler stated that there was a wild raccoon in the neighborhood that probably caused the damage Ann Potter blamed on Lady.

She continued her testimony:

"Later that day, at the time Ann Potter's geese were honking, I was walking Lady past her house. I remember thinking that there must have been a raccoon in the Potters' yard. Lady always barks when she smells a raccoon.

"The barking Ann Potter heard was from Lady, all right. But I was walking her on a leash outside the Potters' house.

"Mrs. Potter phoned me when she found her goose was injured. She yelled at me over the phone, using terrible language.

"When she hung up I went into her backyard. I saw animal tracks in the yard. One set were the tracks Lady had made when she ran there and back earlier that morning.

"But I saw some other prints that looked like they could have been a raccoon's. So I hurried home and brought back my camera. I took a picture of the prints."

This photograph is entered as EXHIBIT C. Note the four-pointed prints that Norma Winkler admits are Lady's. The darker five-pointed prints are those of another animal, possibly a raccoon.

Norma Winkler continued her testimony:

"You see those prints? A raccoon could have easily gone through the fence and attacked the geese. How can Ann Potter say it was my dog? She can't make me pay for the damage because

Lady wasn't responsible. My Lady is a lady!"

LADIES AND GENTLEMEN OF THE JURY:
You have just heard the Case of the Barking Dog. You must decide the merits of Ann Potter's claim. Be sure to carefully examine the evidence in EXHIBITS A, B, and C.

Was Lady responsible for the backyard damage? Or did a wild raccoon do it?

EXHIBIT A

EXHIBIT B

EXHIBIT C

VERDICT

A RACCOON DID THE DAMAGE.

In EXHIBIT C, one of the dark five-pointed prints of the raccoon is on top of a crushed feather. This means the raccoon stepped on Hugo's feather *after* he had lost his tail.

One of the prints of Lady is underneath a feather. Lady must have left the yard *before* Hugo lost his tail feathers.

The Case of
the Filbert Flub

LADIES AND GENTLEMEN OF THE JURY:

When a person obtains something valuable by means of trickery, it is the same as stealing.

Keep this in mind as you decide the case before you today.

Otis Oats, the plaintiff, is suing his neighbor Brad Sweeny for tricking him into giving up a rare postage stamp. Brad Sweeny, the defendant, claims that Oats is mistaken. The rare stamp had been in his collection for years.

Otis Oats has testified as follows:

"I had just returned from visiting my Aunt Emma in Urbanville. She gave me an old family chest to keep. It had lots of old letters and postcards in it.

"When I got home, I looked through the chest. The stamps on the envelopes seemed kind of unusual. I thought some might be valuable. That's when I phoned Brad. His hobby is stamp collecting. It all started when his grandmother gave him her collection years ago. I figured if anyone would know about my stamps, it would be Brad."

The two friends went through the envelopes. After examining them carefully, Brad Sweeny told Oats the stamps weren't worth any more than they had been the day they were printed.

Otis Oats continued his testimony:

"I was disappointed. I told Brad to help himself to any stamps he wanted. He took an envelope that had a stamp with a picture of Filmore Filbert, the inventor of the supernail."

Several months later, Otis Oats read in a newspaper that Sweeny had sold his entire stamp collection, including a very rare stamp worth thousands of dollars. The newspaper had a picture of this stamp.

Oats was very upset. The stamp looked exactly like the one he had given Brad Sweeny, and which Sweeny had told him was worthless.

The envelope with the stamp attached, which Oats says he gave to Sweeny, has been entered as EXHIBIT A.

The Filmore Filbert stamp is known by collectors as the "Filbert flub." When it was originally printed, the artist accidentally drew an extra finger on Filbert's left hand.

The mistake was quickly caught, the hand redrawn, and new stamps printed. But some "Filbert flubs" were already in circulation. Today the "Filbert flub" is very valuable.

A close-up of this rare stamp appears as EXHIBIT B. Filmore Filbert is pictured holding his supernail, a nail that can be hammered into anything. You will note the six fingers on Filbert's left hand.

Otis Oats explained to the court why he is certain the rare stamp is his:

"I visited Brad Sweeny's house lots of times. He was proud of his stamp collection and he always showed it to me. In fact, I got a little bored from seeing it so much. But Brad never showed me the "Filbert flub" stamp. If it were so valuable, he would have been proud to show it to me."

Otis Oats claims that Brad Sweeny took the envelope he gave him with the "Filbert flub" stamp and erased the address. Over it, Sweeny wrote the name and address of his own grandmother, Nora Sweeny. That way Sweeny could say the letter with the rare stamp was addressed to her.

Brad Sweeny says that Otis Oats is mistaken. He explained to the court how he got the rare stamp:

"That's my grandmother's name and address on the envelope. She gave it to me. Grandma was a serious stamp collector. She began collecting in 1920, when she was only ten years old. She was even written up in the newspapers."

Brad Sweeny showed as EXHIBIT C an article describing his grandmother's collection.

A crime lab expert was called in to examine the envelope with the stamp. A special method of chemical analysis was used. Because the envelope was very old, the laboratory expert was unsure whether the original name and address were erased.

Brad Sweeny continued his testimony:

"Even if there were eraser marks, it doesn't prove anything. The letter was addressed in pencil and the person sending it to my grandmother could have made a mistake in her address, erased it, and corrected the mistake."

LADIES AND GENTLEMEN OF THE JURY:

You have just heard the Case of the Filbert Flub. You must decide the merits of Otis Oats's claim. Be sure to carefully examine the evidence in EXHIBITS A, B, and C.

Was the stamp that Brad Sweeny sold from his own collection? Or was it the stamp Otis Oats gave him?

EXHIBIT A

EXHIBIT C

THE DAILY NEWS FEB. 8, 1950

LIBRARY FEATURES STAMP COLLECTION

The Madison Public Library will have an exhibit of the stamp collection of local resident Mrs. Nora Sweeny.

NORA SWEENY

Her collection includes hundreds of unusual stamps, including several that are quite rare.

Mrs. Sweeny has been collecting stamps since she was a youngster.

"I got interested in stamps when I was ten years old, some thirty years ago," said Sweeny. "The library asked if they could be displayed for the townsfolk to see. I think it's a wonderful idea."

Mrs. Sweeny has shown her collection at many antiquarian exhibits in the state.

Library hours are 9 a.m. to 5 p.m. Closed on Sundays.

VERDICT

SWEENY TRICKED OATS INTO GIVING HIM THE STAMP.

The envelope with the Filmore Filbert stamp in EXHIBIT A is addressed to Sweeny's grandmother, Mrs. Nora Sweeny. The date on the envelope shows it was mailed in 1920.

But Sweeny testified that his grandmother began collecting stamps in 1920 when she was only ten years old.

That means Nora was ten years old when the letter was mailed. She wouldn't have been a "Mrs." then, and she would have had her unmarried last name.

Brad Sweeny erased the name on the envelope Otis Oats gave him and substituted his grandmother's name. But he forgot she was too young to be Mrs. Nora Sweeny.

YOU BE THE JURY

Courtroom IV

. . . for Robby, again . . . .

Order in the Court

LADIES AND GENTLEMEN OF THE JURY:
This court is now in session. My name is Judge John Dennenberg. You are the jury, and the trials are set to begin.

You have a serious responsibility. Will the innocent be sent to jail and the guilty go free? Let's hope not. Your job is to make sure that justice is served.

Read each case carefully. Study the evidence presented and then decide.

GUILTY OR NOT GUILTY??

Both sides of the case will be presented to you. The person who has the complaint is called the *plaintiff*. He or she has brought the case to court. If a crime is involved, the State is the accuser.

The person being accused is called the *defendant*. The defendant is pleading his or her innocence and presents a much different version of what happened.

IN EACH CASE, THREE PIECES OF EVIDENCE WILL BE PRESENTED AS EXHIBITS A, B, AND C. EXAMINE THE EXHIBITS VERY CAREFULLY. A *CLUE* TO THE SOLUTION OF EACH CASE WILL BE FOUND THERE. IT WILL DIRECTLY POINT TO THE INNOCENCE OR GUILT OF THE ACCUSED.

Remember, each side will try to convince you that his or her version is what actually happened. BUT YOU MUST MAKE THE FINAL DECISION.

The Case of the Unhappy Hunter

LADIES AND GENTLEMEN OF THE JURY:

If a person is injured on someone else's land, the property owner is responsible. But if people are warned to stay away, the owner is not liable.

This is the point of law you must consider today.

Brendan Mosby, the plaintiff, is suing Hector Peebles for failing to warn hunters that there were dangerous animal traps on his land. Mr. Peebles, the defendant, says that he had posted warning signs to keep people away.

On January 4, Brendan Mosby skipped work to go hunting in Mountain Lakes. The area is located 20 miles outside of Bedford. Each year, hundreds of persons go there to hunt pheasants.

Despite a full day in Mountain Lakes, Mosby was disappointed. He failed to hunt down a single bird.

Mr. Mosby explained to the court how he entered Hector Peebles's property:

"I'd been hunting all day. Early in the afternoon it began snowing real hard. I was growing tired. After hunting for hours, I had hardly seen any pheasants. I was disgusted and decided to go home.

"When I started walking back to my car, I couldn't find the main road. Suddenly I realized I was lost. I got a little scared.

"I must have roamed through Mountain Lakes for over an hour. Finally it stopped snowing. I spotted some telephone poles in the distance. I figured I must be near the main road."

Mosby headed for the road, but he did not realize he was walking through the private property owned by Hector Peebles.

The plaintiff enters as EXHIBIT A a diagram of his location. Peebles's land is in the shaded area.

Mr. Mosby was asked to describe his accident. First the question and then his answer:

Q: Didn't you know you were trespassing on Peebles's land?

A: How could I? There were no signs. I just figured I was walking through the Mountain Lakes hunting area.

Q: Will you tell the court how you were injured?

A: I saw the telephone poles in the distance and headed in their direction. I walked through what I thought was a snow-covered path. Suddenly I felt something sharp clamp tightly around my left leg. It cut into it, and I fell to the ground. Blood started seeping through my pants leg. The pain was terrible.

Q: How did you manage to free yourself?

A: I was really dazed by the pain. But I had enough strength to pry open the jaws of the trap around my leg.

Q: Did you see any signs on the property that warned of animal traps?

A: No. Definitely not. There were no signs on the land.

Brendan Mosby is suing Hector Peebles for medical expenses from his injury and for the pain and suffering it caused. He says that if the land had been properly marked, he never would have walked into the trap.

Mr. Peebles claims that the plaintiff was mistaken. He had posted warning signs all over his property. Brendan Mosby should have seen them.

Peebles testified as follows:

"When I bought the land twelve years ago, the first thing I did was build a wire fence around it. It kept out hunters. And most of all, I didn't want any animals ruining my garden.

"But sometimes an animal would break through my fence, so I put in traps to catch them.

"I check the fence regularly. The afternoon of Mosby's accident, I saw that a section of my fence was down. I would have fixed it then and there, but it started to snow real hard. I thought it could wait until the following day."

Mr. Peebles entered as EXHIBIT B a photo of the broken fence. The footprints show where Brendan Mosby entered Peebles's property.

"If Mosby had been careful, he would have seen my sign. It warns trespassers of my animal traps. I post signs near every trap."

After Mosby was injured, Peebles took a photograph of the area. This is entered as EXHIBIT C. It shows the trap and the warning sign on a nearby tree.

Mr. Peebles continued his testimony:

"I can't be responsible for Mosby's accident. There was enough daylight for him to see my sign. Brendan Mosby walked on my property — plain and simple. He was too lazy to walk around it to reach the main road.

"Mosby never should have been on my land. It was his own carelessness that caused the accident."

LADIES AND GENTLEMEN OF THE JURY: You have just heard the Case of the Unhappy Hunter. You must decide the merits of Brendan Mosby's claim.

Is Hector Peebles responsible for Mosby's injury? Or should the hunter have seen the warning sign?

EXHIBIT A

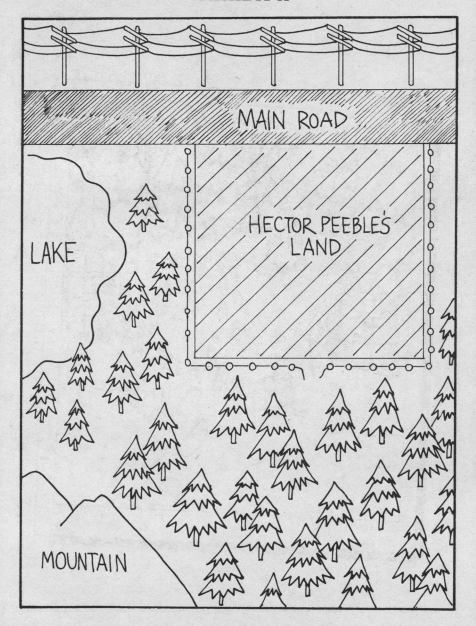

EXHIBIT C

VERDICT

HECTOR PEEBLES IS RESPONSIBLE.

Peebles put up the sign after the accident occurred.

The place where Mosby was injured is shown in EXHIBIT C. The tree limbs are covered with snow. But there is no snow on top of the warning sign. Peebles must have nailed it to the tree *after* it stopped snowing.

The Case of the Exploding Tire

LADIES AND GENTLEMEN OF THE JURY:
When a person buys a product, often she or he is given a written warranty. This guarantees that the product is of good quality.

Sometimes a warranty is written to limit the seller's responsibility. This is called a *limited warranty*. It describes exactly what the seller will do if the product is faulty.

Molly Kramer, the plaintiff, is in court today and claims her car was damaged because of a tire she bought from Ernie's Tire and Auto Center.

Ernie Walker, the defendant, agrees to replace the tire. But he refuses to pay for anything else.

Molly Kramer explained to the court how the damage occurred:

"I own a fifteen-year-old Penza. It's a great car, but the front tires were worn pretty badly. And replacement tires are so expensive these days. When I heard about a tire sale at Ernie's, I drove right over.

"The sale seemed like a bargain, so I bought two new ones. It must have taken about a half

281

hour to replace both tires. I had some work done on my engine, too.

"About a week later, while I was driving home from work, I heard a loud bang. My car jerked to the side of the road. It was really scary."

Miss Kramer got out of her car and inspected the front end. Her new right tire was a rubbery blob.

The new tire had exploded, and the car's front fender was blown partly off. She phoned Ernie Walker and had him tow her car to his garage.

The plaintiff is suing Ernie Walker to replace the tire. She also wants him to pay for the cost of a new front fender.

Molly Kramer continued her testimony:

"When I demanded that Ernie pay for all costs, he refused. He said that he was responsible only for replacing the blown-out tire. I would have to pay for the fender myself.

"Ernie showed me a copy of the bill with a tire warranty printed on the bottom. But I never saw the bill before. It had my signature on it. Ernie must have faked it.

"He must have copied my name on the bill from my signature on the check I gave him."

Molly Kramer's check was entered as EXHIBIT A.

Ernie Walker told his side of the story to the court:

"I warned Miss Kramer that her car was in bad shape and that the wheels needed to be aligned. I tried to convince the lady to get it fixed.

"When she refused, I pointed out the limited warranty to Miss Kramer and had her sign the bill. I gave her a copy to keep."

EXHIBIT B is Ernie Walker's copy of the bill with the tire warranty that has Molly Kramer's signature. Note the wording of the limited warranty.

The defendant claims that his only responsibility is to replace Molly Kramer's tire. He refuses to pay for anything else and says she should contact the tire manufacturer if she isn't satisfied.

A garage worker, Chester Snibbe, saw Ernie give the warranty to Molly Kramer. He took the stand to testify.

Under questioning, Chester said he remembered the woman's visit very clearly:

Q: Where were you when Ernie Walker gave the warranty to the plaintiff?

A: I was replacing a bulb inside the lady's car. Miss Kramer and Ernie were standing in the repair area by the desk.

Q: Did you actually see Ernie hand her the warranty?

A: Sure I did. I was in the front seat fixing the bulb. Ernie had been working under the hood, adjusting the engine. He kept the motor running so he could keep an eye on things in case something went wrong. I saw Ernie fill out the warranty bill and then saw Miss Kramer sign it.

Q: Are you certain?

A: Sure, I'm certain. The warranty forms are on Ernie's desk in the repair area. After she signed it, Ernie kept the white copy and gave a yellow one to Miss Kramer. She put it in her purse.

Q: Did she ask Ernie any questions about the warranty?

A: Not that I know of. Ernie was still checking the engine when I left. I don't know what they talked about.

Q: Did the garage have any signs posted, warning customers of the limited warranty?

A: Sure. There is a sign near the desk in the repair area.

EXHIBIT C is the repair area in Ernie's garage. It shows where the notice is posted on the wall. Questioning of Chester Snibbe continued:

Q: Look at the door next to the sign. Is it possible the door was open and covered the notice?

A: I don't remember. I think the door was closed. But anyway, I saw Miss Kramer sign the warranty. I think that should be good enough.

LADIES AND GENTLEMEN OF THE JURY:
You have just heard the Case of the Exploding Tire. You must decide the merits of the plaintiff's claim. Be sure to carefully examine the evidence in EXHIBITS A, B, and C.

Was Molly Kramer given a limited warranty? Or was the testimony against her a lie?

EXHIBIT A

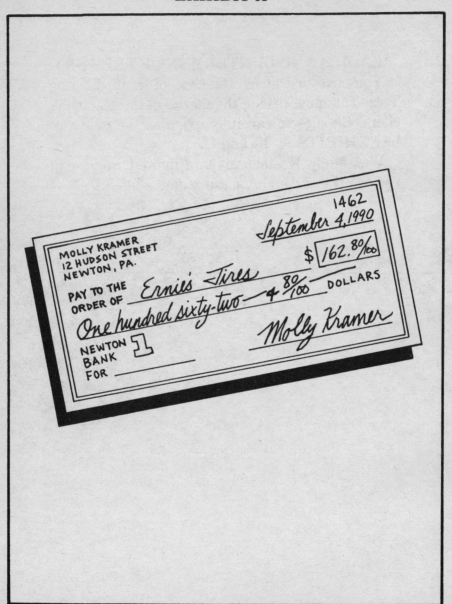

EXHIBIT B

ERNIE'S
TIRE AND AUTO CENTER

NAME __MOLLY KRAMER__ DATE __SEPT. 4, 1990__

ADDRESS __12 HUDSON ST.__ CAR __'74 PENZA__

__NEWTON, PA__

DESCRIPTION

-2 185 16 TCL TIRES, BLACK
@ 58.40 ———— #116.⁸⁰

— TIRE MOUNTING + WHEEL BALANCE— #36.⁰⁰

—ADJUST IDLING ———— #10.⁰⁰

PAID E.W.   TOTAL — #162.⁸⁰

LIMITED WARRANTY

WITHIN 12 MONTHS, IF A TIRE BECOMES UNSERVICEABLE DUE TO WORKMANSHIP OR MATERIAL, THE TIRE WILL BE REPLACED AT NO CHARGE OWNER PAYS FOR MOUNTING AND BALANCING.

DEALER IS NOT RESPONSIBLE FOR ANY OTHER LOSS, INCONVENIENCE OR DAMAGE WHETHER DIRECT, INDIRECT OR CONSEQUENTIAL.

Molly Kramer

287

EXHIBIT C

VERDICT

THE TESTIMONY WAS A LIE.

EXHIBIT C shows the desk where Chester Snibbe claimed Ernie and Miss Kramer were standing. While it was being repaired, Miss Kramer's car would have been parked in *front* of the desk.

Chester never could have seen Molly Kramer at the desk, signing the warranty. He was sitting in the front seat of her car, but the hood of the car was *up*, blocking his view. All Chester could have seen was the car hood.

The Case of the Counterfeit Shopper

LADIES AND GENTLEMEN OF THE JURY:
Distributing fake money is a criminal offense. It is punishable by a long jail sentence.

The federal government, represented by the district attorney, has charged Gilbert Nelson with buying merchandise using counterfeit money.

Mr. Nelson, the defendant, claims he is innocent. He says that it was another shopper who passed the counterfeit bills.

A security guard for Appleby's Department Store was called to the stand:

"My name is Jed Archer, and I have been a security guard with Appleby's for twenty-four years.

"I was at my station on the second floor when Rhonda, the cashier in the coat department, frantically waved in my direction.

"She showed me seven $10 bills that a customer had just given her. He had used them to buy a raincoat. She said the bills seemed funny.

"I examined them closely. They were all brand-new and looked real. But when I ran my thumb across their faces, they just didn't feel right."

EXHIBIT A is a close-up photograph of one of the $10 bills. A crime laboratory has identified it as counterfeit. Note how it compares with a genuine $10 bill. Lines on the outer margin and scroll of the fake bill are blurred and uneven.

Mr. Archer continued his testimony:

"Rhonda pointed across the floor at the man who had just given her the money. He was walking toward the down escalator. I yelled for him to stop. When he heard my voice, the man broke through the crowd and began to run.

"Appleby's Department Store has a steep escalator leading from the second floor to the main floor below. I had to think fast. I pushed the escalator button and switched the stairs so they moved upwards, in the opposite direction.

"Switching the direction of the escalator was a great idea. But the shopper was too quick. He ran down the steps faster than the escalator steps moved up. I chased, but couldn't catch him.

"By the time I was halfway down the steps, the counterfeiter had reached the main floor. He darted out the front door."

The security guard stopped the escalator and telephoned the police.

When officers arrived, they examined the area. A man's wallet was discovered on an escalator step.

EXHIBIT B shows where the wallet was found. An "X" marks the spot. The police believe it was dropped by the criminal during his escape.

Credit cards inside the wallet identified its owner. The wallet belonged to Gilbert Nelson. On this basis, Nelson was arrested. He is charged here today with passing counterfeit money.

Mr. Nelson states that the wallet is his, but he was not involved in the crime. He testified as follows:

"I'm innocent! Sure, I was shopping in Appleby's Department Store that afternoon. But I was nowhere near the coat department.

"There was a lot of yelling going on, and I saw it all happening. I heard the guard shout and run down the escalator. In fact, everyone in the store stopped to see what was going on."

Gilbert Nelson was questioned by the district attorney:

Q: How did your wallet get on the escalator steps?

A: It must have fallen out of my back pocket when I walked down the escalator. But that was after the counterfeiter fled. I left the department store about ten minutes later.

Q: The security guard testified that he stopped the escalator after the criminal escaped. The steps weren't moving. Why didn't you take an elevator instead of walking down the escalator?

A: It might have been easier, but it would have been slower. I was in a hurry. There were long lines at the elevators.

Q: Exactly where were you shopping?

A: I was at the necktie counter on the second floor. I never went near the coat department.

Q: Then how do you account for the counterfeit $10 bills in your wallet?

A: They must have been given to me as change by the clerk at the necktie counter. I remember giving her a $50 bill. The tie cost $9.95. She gave me change of a nickel and four $10 bills.

EXHIBIT C is Gilbert Nelson's wallet, discovered on the escalator steps. The four $10 bills in it have been shown to be counterfeit.

Mr. Nelson's lawyer claims that the counterfeiter could have used fake bills at the necktie counter first, before shopping in the coat department.

These were the counterfeit bills that the necktie clerk took from her cash register and gave to Gilbert Nelson as change.

LADIES AND GENTLEMEN OF THE JURY: You have just heard the Case of the Counterfeit Shopper. You must decide the merits of the district attorney's accusation. Be sure to carefully examine the evidence in EXHIBITS A, B, and C.

Was Gilbert Nelson the man who passed the fake bills? Or was he mistaken for the counterfeiter?

EXHIBIT A

GENUINE BILL

COUNTERFEIT BILL

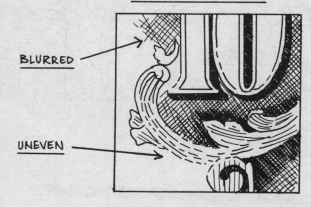

BLURRED

UNEVEN

EXHIBIT C

VERDICT

GILBERT NELSON WAS INNOCENT.

While the counterfeiter was fleeing, the escalator was switched so the steps moved upwards.

If it had been the criminal's wallet that had dropped, the escalator would have carried it to the *top* step.

EXHIBIT B shows where Gilbert's wallet was found. It is on the *bottom* step of the escalator. This means Gilbert had walked down the steps after the counterfeiter had fled and the escalator was stopped.

The Case of the Newspaper Photograph

LADIES AND GENTLEMEN OF THE JURY:

If a newspaper reports that a person committed a crime and the article is false, the wronged person can sue. Printing inaccurate information is known as *libel*.

Glen Baxter, the plaintiff, accuses the *Daily Blaze* of falsely printing a news story that said he was arrested for robbery.

Lawyers for the *Daily Blaze* argue that the newspaper should not be blamed for the wrong information.

Mr. Baxter, a shoe store owner, testified as follows:

"Glen Baxter is my name, and I'm very, very upset. Let me tell you how this whole mix-up started.

"I was standing outside my store on Tilgman Street when I heard a woman scream that her purse had been stolen. I turned around and saw her point at a man. He was running the other way.

"I quickly ran after the thief and chased him down the street."

Baxter gained on the suspect. With one swift spurt, he lunged at the thief and wrestled him to the ground.

"After I tackled him, I held his hands tightly behind his back. A large crowd gathered, and I shouted for someone to call the police."

A nearby police car answered the call. A policeman broke through the crowd and arrested the thief. As Mr. Baxter handed him over, a flash went off at the rear of the crowd. A reporter for the *Daily Blaze* had taken a picture of the arrest.

Glen Baxter continued his testimony:

"Other policemen arrived. I didn't want to be involved. As soon as the purse snatcher was arrested, I quickly slipped into the crowd."

The next day, when the plaintiff read a report of the robbery in the *Daily Blaze*, he was shocked to see a picture of himself standing with the thief and the arresting policeman. But the caption under the picture wrongly identified Glen Baxter as the purse snatcher.

EXHIBIT A is the newspaper article that reported the arrest. Baxter, wearing a white shirt, is described as the thief.

Mr. Baxter claims that the *Daily Blaze*'s mistake caused a loss of business for his shoe store.

"I moved to this town about a year ago. After

I bought the store, business started to improve. But when the picture appeared, customers started avoiding me. They began shopping at another shoe store downtown."

Glen Baxter is suing the *Daily Blaze* for his lost business and for damaging his reputation. Even though the newspaper printed a correction, many people never read it. They still think of him as a thief.

Walter Tubb, a reporter for the *Daily Blaze*, took the stand.

"This is all a terrible mistake. I was the one who took the picture. But it was a policeman who gave me the wrong information. The police are the ones to blame, not my newspaper."

Mr. Tubb testified as follows. First the question and then his answer:

Q: Did you write the caption under the picture?
A: Sure, I admit to it. But I got the information from a policeman at the crime scene. I wrote the picture's caption from my notes.
Q: What did the policeman say?
A: He told me about the robbery and that the person standing on the arresting policeman's right had stolen a lady's purse. The other man on the policeman's left had caught him.

The thief was later identified as Harry Hooper.

He is a known criminal with a prior history of petty theft. Hooper's police record appears as EXHIBIT B.

Walter Tubb's questioning continued:

Q: Could you have been mistaken? Is it possible that in the confusion you wrote down the wrong information?

A: Absolutely not. I'm certain of it. I'm positive I was told that the robber was standing on the policeman's right.

Q: What was the name of the officer who gave you the information?

A: I don't know. With everything going on, I never had time to ask him. I don't think I'd recognize him.

Q: Didn't you see Mr. Baxter leave the crime scene and slip into the crowd after the arrest? Couldn't you have figured out he wasn't the thief?

A: I went back to my office right after I took the picture. I never saw Baxter leave.

Lawyers for the *Daily Blaze* presented EXHIBIT C, a page from Walter Tubb's notebook. It shows how he clearly marked the people in the photograph he had taken. He used these notes to write the caption under the picture.

The *Daily Blaze* argues that the Police Department is to blame. They say that the notes in

Walter Tubb's notebook were copied down directly from a policeman's statement.

Their newspaper has a reputation for being careful, not careless. They ask that the charges against the newspaper be dismissed.

LADIES AND GENTLEMEN OF THE JURY:

You have just heard the Case of the Newspaper Photograph. You must decide the merits of Glen Baxter's claim. Be sure to carefully examine the evidence in EXHIBITS A, B, and C.

Did a policeman give the *Daily Blaze* wrong information? Or was the newspaper at fault?

EXHIBIT A

PURSE SNATCHER ARRESTED

YESTERDAY AFTERNOON, A SUSPECT WAS APPREHENDED WHILE STEALING A WOMAN'S PURSE OUTSIDE STAR'S DEPT. STORE. THE ALLEGED THIEF IS SHOWN ABOVE IN A WHITE SHIRT ON THE ARRESTING POLICEMAN'S RIGHT. HE WAS WRESTLED TO THE GROUND BY THE UNIDENTIFIED MAN ON THE POLICEMAN'S LEFT.

RESIDENT KNOWN
CRIMINAL

NAME: HARRY HOOPER

WHERE BORN: DYSAN, OHIO

SEX: M   AGE: 36   EYES: BROWN

HAIR: BLACK   HEIGHT: 5'10"   WEIGHT: 170 LB.

DISTINCTIVE MARKS AND SCARS: SCAR ON RIGHT CHEEK

REMARKS:

SENTENCE: NY CT. GENERAL SESSION '84 - PETTY THEFT (SUS.)
NY CT. GENERAL SESSION '88 PETTY THEFT (6 MO.)

EXHIBIT C

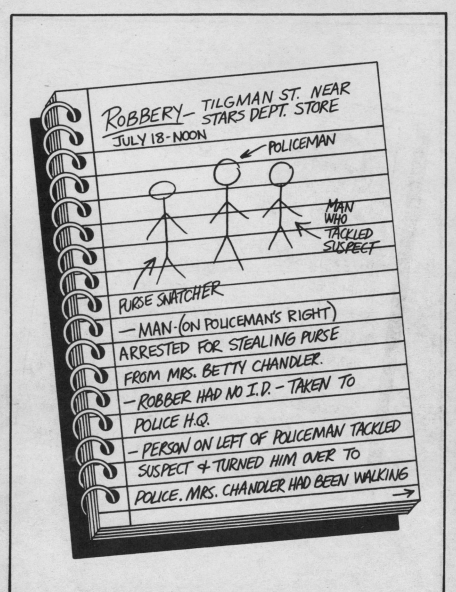

VERDICT

THE *DAILY BLAZE* WAS AT FAULT.

The window sign of Star's Department Store in EXHIBIT A has backward lettering. And the thief's scar is on his left cheek, while in EXHIBIT B it is on his right cheek. This means that the newspaper had printed the picture in *reverse*!

In developing the photograph, the negative was accidentally turned over. Everything in the picture was reversed. The person on the policeman's right was pictured on his left and vice versa.

When the reporter wrote the picture caption from his notes shown in EXHIBIT C, he didn't realize the mistake.

The Case of the Injured Inventor

LADIES AND GENTLEMEN OF THE JURY:
A person can buy an insurance policy that pays expenses if he or she becomes ill and unable to work. This is called *disability insurance.*

The person collects money so long as he or she is too sick to return to work.

Hubert Pickle is suing Writeall Insurance Company for refusing to pay him while he was recovering from an accident. He was bedridden for more than a month.

The insurance company accuses Mr. Pickle of pretending his injury was more serious than it actually was.

Hubert Pickle, the plaintiff, took the stand to explain how his accident occurred.

"Pickle is my name, and I'm president and owner of the Wonderwidgets Company. I invent things that people need but never imagined they could own.

"On July 18, I was testing my latest invention, an electric back scratcher. All of a sudden the machine went wild. It started pounding my back. It almost broke it."

Mr. Pickle claims his back was seriously hurt. He was confined to bed, hardly able to walk.

The attorney for Writeall Insurance questioned Mr. Pickle about his illness:

Q: How long were you confined to bed?

A: About six weeks. I'm asking the insurance company to pay me six weeks of disability insurance. They owe me $3,000.

Q: How did you care for yourself during this period?

A: I could barely get out of bed. My next-door neighbor visited me every morning. She would bring over my meals. She even arranged to move my bed downstairs so I could watch TV all day.

Q: Where is your Wonderwidgets Company located?

A: It's in my house. You see, I *am* the company. My laboratory is in the basement.

Q: Did you try to walk downstairs to your laboratory during the six weeks?

A: Sure I tried, but couldn't. I was eager to get back to work. I had just invented a nonstop waterfall that won a science award. I wanted to make a larger version to generate electricity. It's a solution to the energy crisis!

EXHIBIT A is this amazing waterfall. If you trace your finger along the water, you can see that it always flows downstream. The water can circulate forever.

The lawyer for the insurance company claims Hubert Pickle was faking the seriousness of his injury to collect insurance money. He says the inventor could have returned to his laboratory much earlier.

A private investigator, hired by Writeall, explained why the insurance company refuses to pay:

"My name is Walter Niff. I'm hired by Writeall Insurance Company whenever they think an injury is suspicious. They want me to find out if it's real or not.

"I was assigned to the Pickle case. He had taken out a disability policy with the company.

"I was sitting in my parked car, across the street from Hubert Pickle's house. His shades were pulled down. He even had shades on his basement windows. I watched his house for several hours.

"As I was about to leave, I saw smoke rising from the chimney on top of his house.

"I figured that Mr. Pickle had lit a fire in his fireplace. If he was strong enough to get out of bed, put some logs in the fireplace, and light them, he was able to go down to his laboratory."

When the investigator saw the smoke, he knocked

on Pickle's door. A voice answered. A few minutes later, Hubert Pickle opened the door.

The defense entered as EXHIBIT B a photograph of Pickle's living room as it appeared when Walter Niff was shown into the house.

The insurance investigator continued his testimony:

"Mr. Pickle looked like he was in a lot of pain. He said he barely had enough strength to get out of bed. He said he braced himself on the chair and struggled over to the door to open it for me.

"When I asked Mr. Pickle how he lit the fireplace, the inventor had an explanation. He had invented a remote control device that could light the fireplace while he was still in bed. He called it a Zaplighter.

"I asked Pickle to show me how it worked. He began fidgeting with the device. It was supposed to send an invisible current across the room. When it hit a log, it would start a fire.

"But when I checked the Zaplighter on another log, it wouldn't work. I even tried it up close. The invention was a fake. Hubert Pickle must have grabbed one of the gadgets around his house and pretended it was a Zaplighter."

The defense entered as EXHIBIT C a photograph of the remote control device. It shows the insurance investigator trying to light a log with the invention.

Writeall Insurance believes Hubert Pickle faked

his illness. He wasn't nearly as sick as he pretended to be. They claim he was well enough to walk over to the fireplace, put on some logs, and bend down to light them.

LADIES AND GENTLEMEN OF THE JURY: You have just heard the Case of the Injured Inventor. You must decide the merits of Hubert Pickle's claim. Be sure to carefully examine the evidence in EXHIBITS A, B, and C.

Should Hubert Pickle collect the full disability insurance? Or did he pretend to be sicker than he really was?

EXHIBIT A

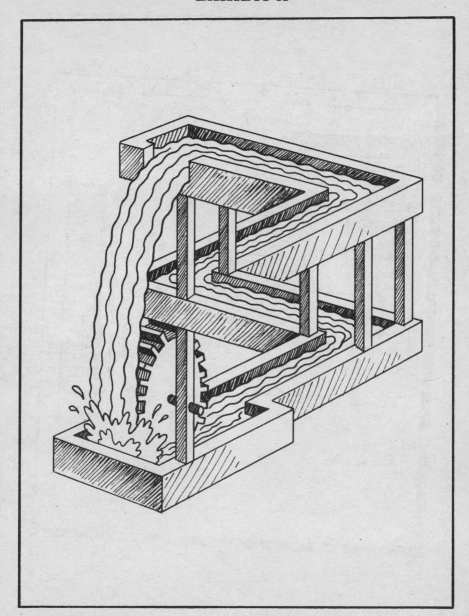

EXHIBIT B

EXHIBIT C

VERDICT

HUBERT PICKLE FAKED HIS DISABILITY.

Pickle claimed that he barely could get out of bed to open the door. He had to brace himself on the chair.

In EXHIBIT B, the corner of the bedsheet is turned down on the side nearest the fireplace. If Pickle had been in bed when the investigator knocked, he would have gotten out on the side by the door.

Pickle had been out of bed when the investigator arrived. He had started the fire. Pickle pretended to be sicker than he really was.

The Case of the
Red Balloons

Ladies and gentlemen of the jury:
A person who helps someone commit a crime
is called an *accessory*. If he or she is found guilty,
an accessory can be punished by the court.

The town of Clemens, represented by the district attorney, accuses Woody Baker of being an
accessory in operating a dishonest game at the
Clemens Carnival. People who played the game
were cheated out of their money.

Mr. Baker, the defendant, says he never was
near the faked game and is being wrongly accused
of the crime.

The Clemens Carnival is the town's major event
of the year. It features top-name entertainment
and has rides, sideshows, and games of skill and
chance.

At this year's carnival, one game drew very
large crowds. It had thirty balloons of different
colors. The game operator, later identified as Otto
Merrell, held the balloon strings. Players paid
$1.00 to pick a string from the tangled ends that
hung down below his hand and pull out a balloon.

Prizes were awarded if certain balloons were chosen. The big prize was an expensive watch. It went to the person who pulled out one of the red balloons.

Officer Carlton Dempsy of the Clemens Police Department was called to the stand to testify:

"Everyone has a great time at the carnival except for us. The police work extra hard to manage the crowd of people that flow into town.

"The day after the carnival opened, we got a tip that the balloon game was faked. One woman lost more than $20.00 trying to pick the red balloon. All she ever won was a lot of junk.

"I decided to watch the balloon game myself from the rear of the crowd.

"After a few people lost, the crowd started to thin out. Then a man wearing sunglasses stepped up to try his luck. He gave the game operator a dollar and tugged on a string. Out came a red balloon.

"The man became very excited. He kept on shouting and created a big stir. He yelled that he had just won a wristwatch. New crowds of people lined up to play the balloon game."

Officer Dempsy states that the man who won was a "shill." That's carnival talk for a person who is hired by the game operator to make believe it's easy to win. A shill knows how the fake game works and secretly returns the prize at the end of the day.

Officer Dempsy continued his testimony:

"I kept watching the balloon game after the man with the sunglasses won. Then I pushed through the crowd and headed for the game operator, Otto Merrell. I wanted to take a look at the balloon strings he was holding.

"Merrell saw me coming, grabbed his money, and ran down the midway. He was out of sight before I could catch him."

The district attorney presented EXHIBIT A, which shows how the balloon game is usually faked. The strings tied to the red balloons are folded back and hidden in the game operator's hand. People who play the game never get a chance to pull them.

A short time later, as Officer Dempsy was walking around the carnival grounds, he saw a man who resembled the shill. Although the man was not wearing sunglasses, he looked just like the person who had pulled out the red balloon.

The man was arrested as an accessory to a dishonest carnival game.

The man gave his name as Woody Baker and Hobart Gap as his home town.

The district attorney showed EXHIBIT B, the application form that Otto Merrell filled out when he applied for permission to run the carnival game. Woody Baker came from the same town as Otto Merrell.

Woody Baker took the stand in his own defense.

He claims he is innocent. The policeman made a big mistake.

I quote from his testimony. First the question and then his answer:

Q: Did you know the carnival operator, Otto Merrell?

A: Sure I know him. We come from the same town. He was a shady character. But I haven't seen him for years.

Q: What were you doing in Clemens?

A: The same as everyone else. I went to the carnival. I go every year.

Q: Did you play the balloon game?

A: I never went near any of the games. I just got there and went directly to see my favorite sideshow, the Daredevil Motorcycles.

Q: Is there anyone who saw you at the sideshow?

A: Listen. I don't live in Clemens. I was only visiting. The people at the sideshow were all strangers to me.

Woody Baker says Officer Dempsy has mistaken him for the shill. He asks the court to study the policeman's notebook, which is entered as EXHIBIT C.

"Even his notes say I wasn't wearing sunglasses. The man at the balloon game was. How could he say I looked like that man? Some people are hard to describe when they wear sunglasses."

Woody Baker claims his arrest is a case of mistaken identity. He says he was not involved in the fake carnival game.

LADIES AND GENTLEMEN OF THE JURY:
You have just heard the Case of the Red Balloons. You must decide the merits of the town's accusation. Be sure to carefully examine the evidence in EXHIBITS A, B, and C.

Was Woody Baker involved as an accessory to the dishonest balloon game? Or was the policeman mistaken?

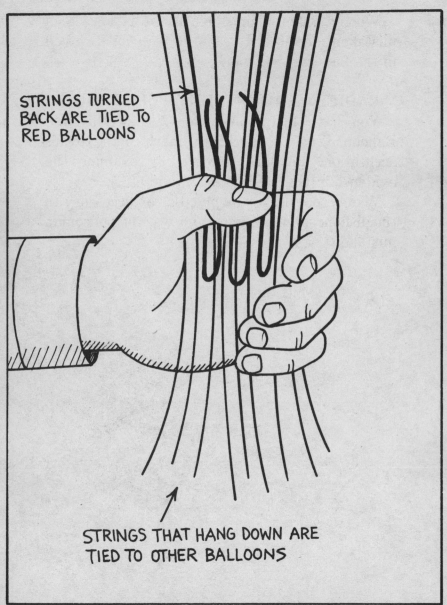

STRINGS TURNED BACK ARE TIED TO RED BALLOONS

STRINGS THAT HANG DOWN ARE TIED TO OTHER BALLOONS

APPLICATION
CARNIVAL BOOTH

NAME: OTTO MERRELL

ADDRESS: 166 FRONT ST.
HOBART GAP, TX.

NATURE OF BOOTH: STRING GAME.
PICK A STRING ATTACHED TO COLORED
BALLOONS. PRIZES GIVEN FOR THE
COLOR BALLOON CHOSEN

IS BOOTH A GAME OF SKILL? NO

SIZE OF BOOTH: 10 FT. X 18 FT.

ELECTRICITY REQUIRED: NO

Otto Merrell
SIGNATURE

EXHIBIT C

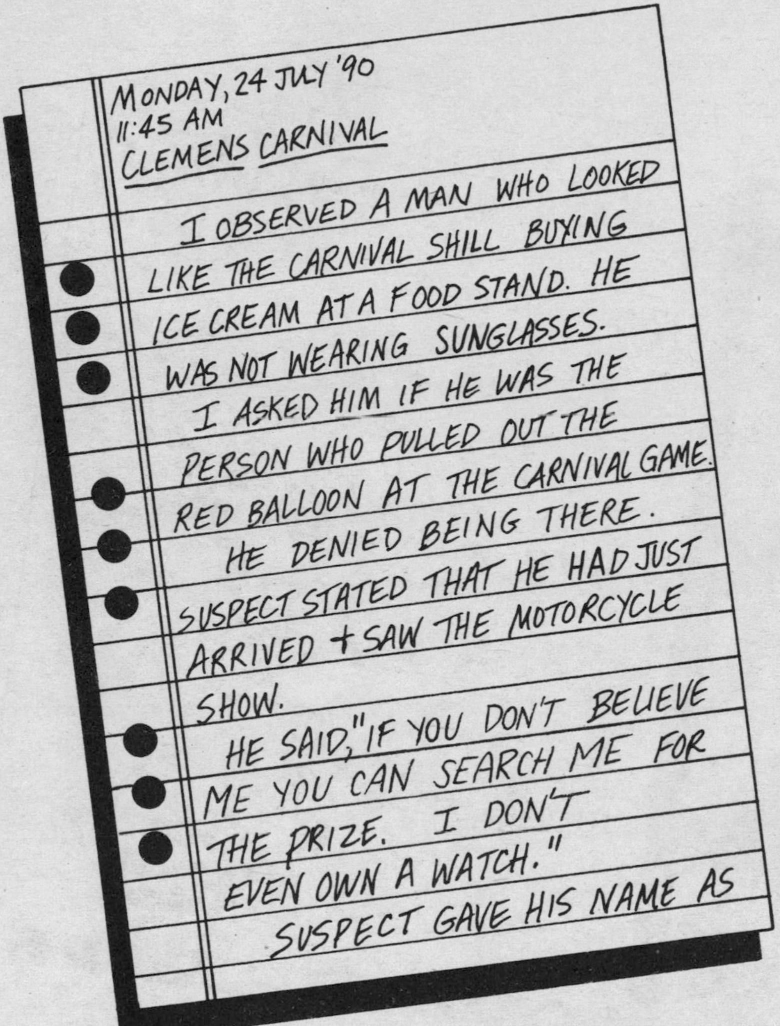

MONDAY, 24 JULY '90
11:45 AM
CLEMENS CARNIVAL

I OBSERVED A MAN WHO LOOKED
LIKE THE CARNIVAL SHILL BUYING
ICE CREAM AT A FOOD STAND. HE
WAS NOT WEARING SUNGLASSES.
I ASKED HIM IF HE WAS THE
PERSON WHO PULLED OUT THE
RED BALLOON AT THE CARNIVAL GAME.
HE DENIED BEING THERE.
SUSPECT STATED THAT HE HAD JUST
ARRIVED + SAW THE MOTORCYCLE
SHOW.
HE SAID,"IF YOU DON'T BELIEVE
ME YOU CAN SEARCH ME FOR
THE PRIZE. I DON'T
EVEN OWN A WATCH."
SUSPECT GAVE HIS NAME AS

VERDICT

WOODY BAKER WAS AN ACCESSORY.

In the policeman's notebook of EXHIBIT C, Baker was asked if he was the person who pulled out the red balloon.

In his reply, Baker claimed he never was near the balloon game. He offered to be searched and told the policeman he didn't even own a watch.

But Baker could not have known that a wristwatch was the prize unless he had been at the fake carnival game.

The Case of the Confusing Candy

Ladies and gentlemen of the jury:
It is against the law to sell a product that purposely can be confused with someone else's. This can happen when one company calls its product by the same name that is already used by another company.

To do so is called *unfair trade practice.*

Bodine Candy Company is suing Marjorie Bodine for selling chocolates under the Bodine name. Ms. Bodine, the defendant, claims her father sold Bodine Chocolates long before Bodine Candy Company ever existed. She says that he was the first to use the Bodine name.

Alfred Pullman, who is president of Bodine Candy Company, has testified as follows:

"I became the president of our company three years ago after our founder, Harold Bodine, retired. We make the chewiest chewing gum in the country.

"Oh, excuse me while I take this gum out of my mouth.

"Our company started in 1975, when Harold Bodine made an important discovery in his kitchen. By mixing together some secret ingredients, he could make a gum that crackled and sparkled when you chewed it.

"If you chewed it in the dark, every time your mouth opened, tiny sparks flew out.

"Harold Bodine called it 'Bodine Chewing Gum' and began selling it through local stores. The gum became popular immediately. Kids kept on asking for Bodine gum.

"Soon demand for the gum spread to neighboring towns. Then orders started rolling in from outside the state. Today the Bodine Candy Company has three plants and warehouses all over the country."

Mr. Pullman continued his testimony:

"Our gum was so popular that we came out with candy corn, coconut bars, licorice, and other candies, all with the Bodine name."

EXHIBIT A is a box of Bodine Jewel Berry Drops. The name is prominently displayed.

"You've heard our slogan, 'Throw in a Bodine and throw out your worries.' Our gum and candies are so delicious, they make people happy."

Bodine Candy Company accuses Marjorie Bodine of using the Bodine name because the company made it famous. The company believes she made up the story about her father selling chocolates before Bodine Candy Company was formed.

The company asks the court to stop her from selling her chocolates in the state. It wants her to change the name because people will confuse it with Bodine products.

As proof of the confusion they enter, as EX-HIBIT B, a box of Bodine Chocolates sold by Marjorie Bodine.

The defendant, Ms. Bodine, claims that she has the right to use the name Bodine. She says that the chocolate recipe was her grandmother's. Her grandmother had left school after the third grade to make chocolates in their family's candy shop in France.

When Marjorie's father, Philip, moved to the United States, he brought boxes of her grandmother's chocolates with him. That was more than twenty years ago. It was five years before Harold Bodine discovered his chewing gum.

Marjorie's father was a door-to-door brush salesman. He decided to make extra money by selling Grandma Bodine's chocolates to his customers. Grandma Bodine sent boxes of her candy to Philip from her shop in France.

Last year, Marjorie Bodine decided to quit her job and sell chocolate candy using her grandmother's recipe. She never knew her grandmother, but found the candy recipe among her father's letters.

Lawyers for the defense called to the stand

Gretchen Potts, who was one of Philip Bodine's customers.

We quote from her testimony. First the question and then her answer:

Q: Did you ever buy anything from Philip Bodine?

A: Oh my, yes. He had the fuzziest brushes. Philip was such a nice man. He didn't speak English very well, but he had the cutest accent.

Q: What else did you buy from him?

A: Oh, you mean the chocolates? Yes, he sold the most delicious chocolate candy.

Q: When you bought the chocolates from Philip Bodine, how were they packaged? Were they in a Bodine Chocolate box?

A: I really can't remember. He always made up a special order for me. Every time he came by to sell me his brushes, I would give him my large silver candy dish. He would return it the next day filled with his delicious chocolates.

Q: Did you ever see the original box of chocolates that he used to fill your silver candy dish? Was it from a candy box that had "Bodine Chocolates" printed on it?

A: Oh, I have such a terrible memory. But I seem to recall that he showed me a candy box one day. I think he said it came from his mother's candy shop.

EXHIBIT C is Marjorie Bodine's chocolate recipe that her grandmother sent to her father.

Marjorie Bodine says she has every right to use the Bodine name on her chocolate candy. Her father used the Bodine name first, years before people ever heard of Bodine Candy Company.

LADIES AND GENTLEMEN OF THE JURY:
You have just heard the Case of the Confusing Candy. You must decide the merits of Bodine Candy Company's claim. Be sure to carefully examine the evidence in EXHIBITS A, B, and C.

Should Marjorie Bodine be allowed to sell Bodine Chocolates? Or did she make up the story about her grandmother's candy?

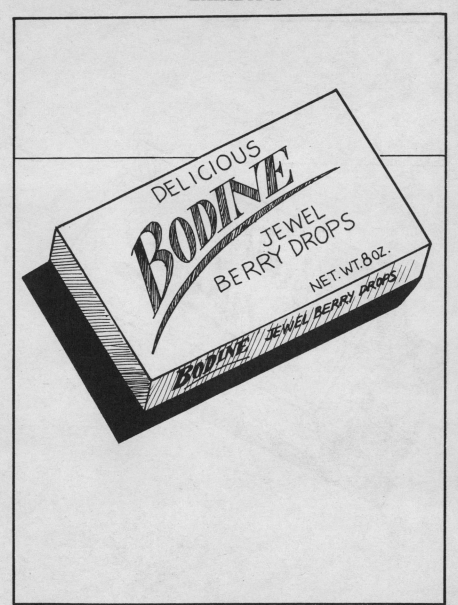

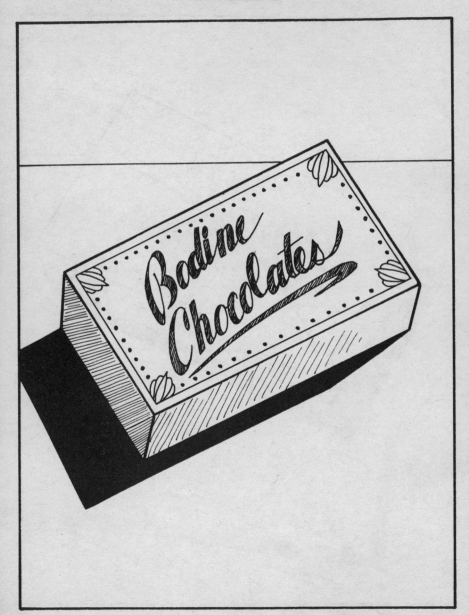

EXHIBIT C

October 5

Dear Philip,

Here is my recipe for my cocoa cones:

Sift one cup sugar
Whip until stiff –
    3 egg whites
    pinch of salt

Slowly mix sugar into the whip.
    Then add:
    2 teaspoons water
    1 teaspoon vanilla

Whip for 5 minutes and add:
    3 tablespoons cocoa

Drop the batter from a spoon into tin. Shape the candy into small cones. Bake until a little dry.

I hope you like my candy recipe. Do not eat too many at one time.

Love
Momma

VERDICT

MARJORIE MADE UP THE STORY ABOUT THE CANDY.

Marjorie claimed her grandmother left school after the third grade to work in the family candy shop in France. And the witness said that her father, Philip, spoke poor English.

The recipe in EXHIBIT C is a fake, written by Marjorie Bodine. If it had been from her grandmother, the recipe would not be in English. It would have been written in French.

The Case of the
Dangerous Dog

LADIES AND GENTLEMEN OF THE JURY:
If a dog bites someone and causes serious injury, the owner is responsible. But if the person bitten was being cruel to the animal, that may be a different matter.

Consider this point of law as you hear the case before you today.

Andy Porter, the plaintiff, is suing for injuries he received when Rita Finch's dog attacked him.

Mrs. Finch, the defendant, claims that her dog is harmless. It bit Andy because he hit the dog with a big stick.

The plaintiff explained to the court how his injury happened:

"My name is Andy Porter. I'm a ninth-grader at Eagle Rock High School. Every morning before class, I deliver newspapers to the people in the Glen Cove section of town. One of the houses is 28 Glen Cove Lane. That's where Mrs. Finch lives.

"About a week before I was bitten, Mrs. Finch

began letting Piper out to play on the front lawn. Piper is a large bulldog.

"Every morning when I delivered the newspaper, the dog would start snarling at me. He had a terrible bark. It was frightening.

"I had to deliver the newspapers to keep my job. So I figured it was safer to throw the paper on Mrs. Finch's lawn and run. I didn't want to get too close to Piper."

On the morning of October 16, when Andy Porter was delivering to the Finch house, Andy claims Piper attacked him. The dog leaped at Andy, biting him on his right arm.

Andy Porter's arm was covered with blood. He flagged down a passing car and was driven to the hospital emergency room. The wound required ten stitches.

When the boy returned home from the hospital, his mother took a photograph of the injury. This is entered as EXHIBIT A.

Andy Porter is suing Piper's owner for medical expenses and his pain and suffering because of the injury.

Andy missed three days of school. He even gave up his delivery route.

The plaintiff continued his testimony:

"When Mrs. Finch began letting Piper out, I phoned her and said I was scared he might bite me. She just laughed. She said I was a sissy, and that I didn't have to be afraid of Piper."

EXHIBIT B is a photograph of the shirt Andy was wearing. It shows more details of the attack. The dog bit through the shirt, making a bloody tear. Andy insists he did nothing to provoke the attack.

In Rita Finch's testimony to the court, she tells a different story. She admits that her dog bit the plaintiff. But she says Piper is harmless. He attacks only when he has a reason.

I will quote from Mrs. Finch's testimony. First the question and then her answer:

Q: Has your dog ever bitten a person before?

A: No, never. He's very well trained. Why, I even gave him lessons at the Ruff Ruff and Tuff Doggie School.

Q: If a burglar broke into your house, do you think Piper would attack?

A: Of course! My dog isn't that timid. The school taught Piper how to be a good watchdog.

Q: Did you see the attack against Andy Porter?

A: Sure I did. But he made my dog do it. The boy swung at Piper with a big stick. Piper was only protecting himself.

Q: How do you know?

A: I had let Piper out on the front lawn and was making breakfast. All of a sudden I heard him barking real loud. Then I heard a whine, like he was hurt. I looked out the window and there was Andy Porter.

337

Q: What was he doing?

A: I saw him pushing Piper with a big stick. I was horrified. All of a sudden, Andy raised the stick high over his head and struck at Piper. My dog dodged the swing and the stick glanced off Piper's tail.

Q: Did you actually see your dog bite the plaintiff?

A: Yes, I saw it all happen. I dashed out the front door as fast as I could. Andy had raised the stick high over his head for another strike. That's when Piper jumped up and bit him.

Q: Andy Porter claims that he never hit Piper. Is there any question in your mind that your dog was protecting himself?

A: The boy is flat out lying. He just doesn't like dogs. Andy told me so over the telephone. He hit Piper because he was afraid of him.

The defense entered as evidence EXHIBIT C. It is the stick Mrs. Finch says Andy Porter was holding. When Piper bit him, the boy dropped it and ran.

Mrs. Finch says the charges against her should be dismissed. Piper attacked Andy because the boy hit him.

LADIES AND GENTLEMEN OF THE JURY: You have just heard the Case of the Dangerous

Dog. You must decide the merits of Andy Porter's claim. Be sure to carefully examine the evidence in EXHIBITS A, B, and C.

Did Andy Porter strike Mrs. Finch's dog? Or did the dog attack him without cause?

EXHIBIT B

EXHIBIT C

VERDICT

ANDY PORTER STRUCK THE DOG.

Piper's bite went through Andy's sleeve and into his arm.

In EXHIBIT A, the dog's bite mark is on the *upper* part of Andy's arm. But the tear in his shirt, in EXHIBIT B, is on the *lower* part of the sleeve.

This could happen only if Andy's arm was raised. Then the lower part of his sleeve would *slide down* his raised arm.

Rita Finch had told the truth. Andy held the stick high over his head to strike her dog. Piper bit him while Andy's arm was in the air.

The Case of the Big Bank Robbery

Ladies and gentlemen of the jury:

To find a person guilty of a crime, you must have sufficient proof that he or she did it.

Keep this in mind as you go over the facts in this case. Since we are in criminal court today, the State is the accuser.

The State, represented by the district attorney, has accused Bret Brewster of robbery. The State believes he is one of two men who held up an armored truck. Police have been unable to locate the other man.

Mr. Brewster, the defendant, has pleaded not guilty and claims his arrest is a mistake.

On the morning of February 16, as the guard for Grinks Protection Service delivered money to Fidelity Bank, he was held up by a masked man.

Edgar Holmes, the guard, described for the court what happened:

"I had just pulled into the bank parking lot. I go there every morning, just before it opens.

"I had put on the brakes and unlocked the truck door. Suddenly the door swung wide open. I found

344

myself staring at the barrel of a long revolver.

"The man pointing it at me was wearing a mask. He told me that if I cooperated, I wouldn't get hurt.

"The robber ordered me to open the back of my truck and hand over the money bags inside."

Edgar Holmes followed the masked man's instructions. The robber handed the bags to a second man who was waiting in a nearby car. Then he jumped in and the two men sped away.

The guard provided police with a description of the robbers:

"The man with the gun was tall — maybe six feet. He was wearing a gray sweater and chinos. The man in the car wore a mask, too. I could see he had a beard."

The robber left a telling clue. When police checked the truck's door handle, they found a set of fingerprints. The prints were identified as those of Frank Paxton, a man with a previous criminal record.

Paxton is the owner of Frank's Pizzeria. After getting a search warrant, police hurried to the pizza store only to find it was closed. A sign was hanging on the front door.

A photograph of the pizza store is entered as EXHIBIT A.

When police knocked on the door, a man opened it. He was eating a baloney sandwich. The man identified himself as Bret Brewster. He was of short, heavy build and had a beard. The owner of the store was nowhere to be found.

Police guarded Bret Brewster as they searched the store. Inside two empty pizza boxes, they found all of the stolen bank money, neatly stacked in packets of crisp hundred-dollar bills.

Brewster was placed under arrest and charged as the bearded man driving the getaway car. Police believe that Bret Brewster had returned to the store and planned to pick up his share of the robbery money.

The police searched Brewster. His wallet contained $73.00. He also had a key to Frank's Pizzeria.

This key is entered as EXHIBIT B.

The State asked Brewster about his association with Frank Paxton:

Q: Is it true that you and Frank Paxton palled around together?

A: Sure, we used to be friends. But for the past year I haven't seen much of him.

Q: Then what were you doing in his store?

A: This sounds strange, but you've got to believe me. I hadn't seen or heard from Frank in months. Then, one day, he phoned long distance and asked for a favor.

Q: Where did he phone from?

A: That's just it. Frank wouldn't say. He just

told me he had to be out of town for a few weeks. He asked me to go over to his pizza store and put out the garbage and check that the oven was shut off. He told me to hang up a CLOSED sign.

Q: How did you get into his store?

A: When he phoned, Frank told me I could pick up his key. He said that he had mailed it to the store, and I would find it when I got there.

Bret Brewster claims the key the police found in his possession belonged to Frank Paxton. Brewster never had one. He went inside the store only to do Paxton a favor.

The defense claims the State does not have sufficient proof that Brewster was a partner to the robbery. The only fingerprints on the pizza boxes were those of Frank Paxton.

This fingerprint report is entered as EXHIBIT C.

The defense argues that the guard's description of the man in the car was not detailed. Hundreds of men in the town have beards.

Bret Brewster's lawyer claims he is innocent. He asks that the charges be dismissed.

LADIES AND GENTLEMEN OF THE JURY:
You have just heard the Case of the Big Bank Robbery. You must decide the merits of the

State's accusation. Be sure to carefully examine the evidence in EXHIBITS A, B, and C.

Was Bret Brewster involved in the holdup? Or did someone else help Frank Paxton steal the bank money?

EXHIBIT A

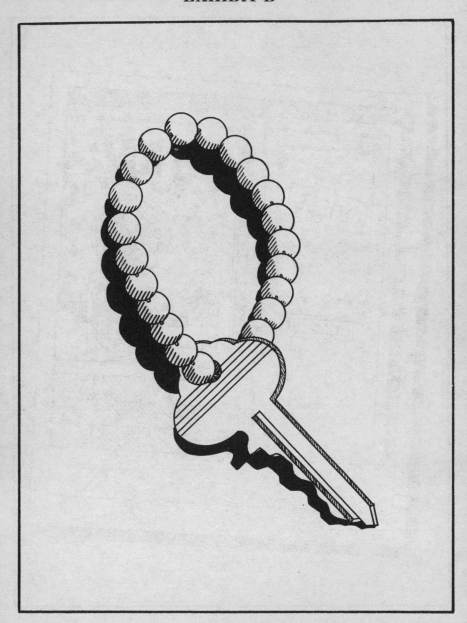

EXHIBIT C

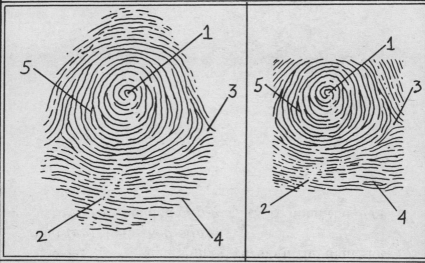

FINGERPRINT REPORT

SOURCE: EMPTY PIZZA BOX
         FRANK'S PIZZERIA

DATE: 2-18-90

PIZZA BOX   FRANK PAXTON

REFERENCE: FRANK PAXTON P-6804

COMPARISON: LATENT PRINT MATCHES FILE PRINT OF
FRANK PAXTON. NOTE THE FOLLOWING:
   1.) WHORL
   2.) SCAR
   3.) DELTA
   4.) ISLAND
   5.) FORK

VERDICT

BRET BREWSTER WAS INVOLVED IN THE HOLDUP.

Brewster claimed that Frank Paxton mailed the key to the pizza store for him to pick up. Brewster said he had no key of his own.

EXHIBIT A shows the mail slot in the door of the pizza store. If Paxton's key arrived by mail, it would have been slipped through the mail slot and *into* the locked store.

Brewster needed *another* key to open the door — his own.

The Case of the Thirsty Helper

LADIES AND GENTLEMEN OF THE JURY:

When a person is hired to work by the hour, she or he is expected to do the job responsibly. Otherwise, the employer does not have to pay in full.

Consider this as you listen to both sides of the case presented to you today.

Donald Breen, the plaintiff, says he overpaid a woman he hired to work for him. She only did half as much work as she should have. But Emily Chowder, the defendant, disagrees.

Mr. Breen recently purchased an old motel located on a main highway. He fixed up the rooms so they looked brand new. A week before the motel opened, Breen planned to send out announcements.

Mr. Breen hired Emily Chowder to help with the mailing. Her job was to take 1,000 announcements, fold and stuff them into envelopes, and paste on stamps.

The two agreed that Emily would be paid $6.00 an hour for the job.

The plaintiff explained to the court why he is suing Emily Chowder:

"It was about eight o'clock in the morning when Miss Chowder arrived at my motel office. She was ready to start the job. I left her alone at the desk while I ran some errands.

"When I got back later that afternoon, Miss Chowder was still at the desk, folding the letters and stuffing them in envelopes. She had finished only half the job.

"The woman said she had been working for eight hours straight. I was surprised she hadn't finished. But I paid her for the eight hours anyway and said I would finish the rest of the job myself."

EXHIBIT A is a photo of Emily Chowder at the desk when Donald Breen returned. Notice the piles of announcements that still need to be stuffed into envelopes.

Mr. Breen continued his testimony.

"I couldn't understand what took her so long until I noticed that the rear door to the office was open. It leads to my motel's swimming pool.

"Suddenly I realized why Miss Chowder had finished only half the job. There, by the edge of the pool, I saw puddles of water.

"Emily Chowder wasn't just stuffing envelopes all day. She did some goofing off, diving and swimming in the pool. The fresh puddles of water prove it."

EXHIBIT B is a photograph of the deep end of the pool where Donald Breen saw the puddles.

Breen was very upset. He timed himself while he stuffed the remaining 500 envelopes. He finished the job in four hours. It had taken Emily eight hours to do the first 500 envelopes.

Mr. Breen is suing to recover the extra money he paid her. He says he should pay the woman only for four hours of work.

Emily Chowder took the stand and described her work to the court. She insisted it really took her the full eight hours.

"I'm a very particular person, you know. I figured Mr. Breen wanted me to do a very neat job, so I was very careful. I neatly folded each announcement before I inserted it.

"Mr. Breen didn't even have a moistener for me. I had to lick the envelopes with my tongue. That took extra time. And the glue tasted just terrible."

Emily Chowder explained to the court why she feels that Breen is mistaken. First the question and then her answer:

Q: Why did Mr. Breen finish the job much faster than you?

A: I think he was trying to prove I was too slow

so he could get some of his money back. I could have done the job a lot faster, too. But it wouldn't have been very neat.

Q: Did you take any time off during the eight hours?

A: No, I didn't even eat lunch. I worked straight through without stopping.

Q: Then how do you account for the puddles around the pool?

A: It's all because I had to lick those envelopes shut. I stopped each time I got real thirsty. My tongue and throat became very dry.

Miss Chowder claimed that she looked around for a water fountain, but couldn't find one. Then she went outside by the pool and found a hose.

Miss Chowder turned on the water several times during the day to drink from the hose. But the last time, just before Mr. Breen returned, she had an accident.

"As I was drinking from the hose, Mr. Breen's dog came running toward me. It knocked the hose right out of my hand. The water sprayed everywhere.

"The water came out so fast that the hose kept on whipping back and forth. When I turned off the water, the whole area was drenched."

The defendant offered as evidence EXHIBIT C. It shows the hose she drank from which was near the motel pool.

Emily Chowder claims that she never swam in Donald Breen's pool. She worked nonstop, except when she got thirsty. She says she is entitled to keep all the money for her eight hours of work.

LADIES AND GENTLEMEN OF THE JURY:
You have just heard the Case of the Thirsty Helper. You must decide the merits of Donald Breen's claim. Be sure to carefully examine the evidence in EXHIBITS A, B, and C.

Did Emily Chowder do a full eight hours work? Or did she take time off to go swimming?

EXHIBIT A

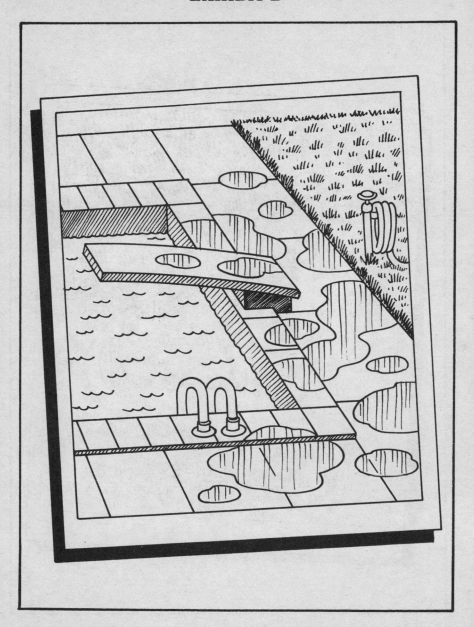

EXHIBIT C

VERDICT

EMILY CHOWDER NEVER WENT INTO THE POOL.

Had Emily swam in the pool, her hair would have been soaked, too. She couldn't possibly have had the neatly styled hair shown in EXHIBIT A.